THE MAGIC PLACES

ELIZABETH JENNER

THE MAGIC PLACES

Arcadia Books Ltd
139 Highlever Road
London W10 6PH
www.arcadiabooks.co.uk

First published in Great Britain 2017
Copyright © Elizabeth Jenner 2017

ISBN 978-1-911350-06-4

Typeset in Garamond by MacGuru Ltd
Printed and bound by TJ International, Padstow PL28 8RW

ARCADIA BOOKS DISTRIBUTORS ARE AS FOLLOWS:

in the UK and elsewhere in Europe:
BookSource
50 Cambuslang Road
Cambuslang
Glasgow G32 8NB

in Australia/New Zealand:
NewSouth Books
University of New South Wales
Sydney NSW 2052

For Mum

THE MAGIC PLACES

1

The Door in the Trees

It might begin with a trip to the shops.

She is there that day, during her lunch break, in the large, bright glassy box of a department shop floor, picking up hand creams and then putting them down again. It is her mother's birthday next week. She wants something special, something that will show her mother she has put in a bit of effort, something that looks expensive, but is not *too* expensive. Something that will be easy to post.

And he is there on this day too, standing in an aisle, looking for a token from this trip for his wife, something that will show her he has put in a bit of effort, something that she will know is expensive. Something that will fit in a suitcase.

They face each other, over a display of floral soaps and French names. And then, as they must do, they both look up.

She sees a familiar face, pulled a little lower by lines and greying hair. A pair of unfamiliar glasses on the recognisable hook of the nose. A dull but neatly fitted suit, on broad shoulders.

Marcus?

He frowns, and she realises that her face, her body, will be less familiar to him. He has not seen her since she was ten, climbing over rocks on a beach, with bramble-scratched arms and a sunburnt nose.

Clare, she says quickly, it's Clare. Josie's daughter.

Those new lines on his face move upwards around his smile, and he is suddenly, again, just as he always was. Clare. God. Clare. How lovely. How are you?

He doesn't even let her reply as he moves sideways and round the stack of bottles towards her. She takes a step towards him and then stops, a tub of something rose-patterned and gilt-edged held too tightly against her chest.

How lovely, he says again, I can't believe it's you. How lovely to see you.

And you, she says. How have you all been? As she says it, she knows that *all* is the wrong word for a family where one will always be missing.

He pauses again, and it seems as if all the noises around them, the clatter of talk and cash registers and tannoy announcements are suddenly harder and brighter than before. This is the wrong place for these words, for this silence between them. She wishes they were somewhere else, somewhere smaller, somewhere darker.

Not too bad, he says eventually, and the clatter recedes into the background again. We're all well. But how are you? How's Josie?

They talk for a few more minutes. She asks after his wife and daughter, and they smooth over the awkward join in the conversation with a few exchanges about the people they each once knew. The dark crack sits beneath them, splitting slowly.

Look, he says then, I really have to go now. I'll be late for my meeting. He takes a breath. The crack widens. But I don't suppose you're free tonight? It would be such a shame to have found you like this and then ... lose you. If you know what I mean. I mean, you probably have plans already, but on the off-chance you don't?

I don't have plans, she says, really, I don't.

Great, he says, great. My hotel's near the station. Is there somewhere around there we could go?

She thinks about sitting in a dingy pub near the station on a Thursday night, trying to talk to this man who had taught her about seaglass and picking strawberries. She resents the idea of half of this conversation being leached away by loud music or excuse-mes or are-you-finished-with-that? However, it still surprises her a little when she says: I'm just one stop up the line from there. Why don't you just come to mine? I'll cook you dinner.

That's very nice of you, he says. Are you sure?

It gives us more of a chance to catch up, she says. After so long. What do you like to eat? How about fish?

That sounds great, he says. Great.

Great, she says, great. And then he laughs at the repetition, and after a second she does too.

See you about seven? Let me take your address.

And just like that, he is coming to her flat for dinner.

So now, just like that, she must stop off at the supermarket on her way home. She lives a life balanced on the delicate equilibrium of the single woman, a steady existence of hard-boiled eggs and single glasses of red wine. She buys packs of two and freezes one for later, measures out the portions of her day in neat plastic Tupperware boxes. She keeps the TV remote in a china dish on the coffee table. She knows how much milk is in the fridge at any given moment. The tangles of other people's habits are left in the pub or the station. Once she steps through that chipped blue door, she is the centre of a world where the books are stacked up on the shelf in exactly the order she has chosen.

It is always a novelty to stalk the aisle of the supermarket thinking in twos, in double portions, treading in the footsteps of somebody else's tastes, edging round allergies and suppositions of likes and dislikes. She thrusts a basket over her arm with purpose.

She has said fish. He has said that sounds great. But does all fish sound great? Or does some fish sound better than others? What is tuna against salmon, coley over mackerel?

There is no accounting for the vagaries of someone else's taste, in the same way that there is no way of predicting the shifts in someone else's mood. She thinks about the negotiations needed to establish the delicate counterbalance of who buys the milk or goes first in the shower. After you, no you, you go first, yes please, if you like, if you want, that is to say if you do want? Is that what you want? Is this what she wants?

She balances the lemon she has picked up on the palm of her hand. It sits in the curve of her thumb as if it belongs there. She puts it into her basket.

And maybe the time it takes to decide these things on behalf of somebody else is not important. Maybe it is perfectly normal to deliberate so long between a cod fillet and a tuna steak. She looks at the fish and they stare back, with glassy, scornful eyes. Does it really matter what she chooses, how soon she makes the decision?

Sorry, I think I'm a little early, he says, if that's all right.

It's all right, she says, yes, yes, it's all right.

She opens the door fully, and presses back against the wall to let him in. He has brought tulips, a tight bunch of stiff red petals in his hand. They seemed like a good idea when he bought them. He remembers feeling the waxy petals in his fingers as he chose them. It would be nice to take her something as a gesture. Of what, he is not sure.

I was just finishing off in here, she says, leading him through to the kitchen. He follows her in. A neat white row of cupboards, a pan bubbling on the hob, a smell of something almost ready. He thrusts the tulips at her. The gesture is too forceful, he is too forceful. She takes them from him, and he finds himself apologising.

No, no, they're lovely, she says, thank you so much. You didn't need to do this.

She lays them down on top of one of the white cupboards and takes his coat, pours him a glass of wine from the bottle in the fridge. He feels easier with the glass in his hand. At her insistence, he sits at her counter and watches her move about the kitchen. She still has the careful and deliberate movements that he recognises from the little girl. They sit better on the adult Clare than they had on the child. He notices she has changed her dress to something dark and flared with prim polka dots. He has removed the tie from his suit.

She pulls apart the cellophane of the tulips with small, neat movements, and they chat, above the rustle of the paper on the counter.

It's a lovely flat you have here.

It's small, but it works for me. I like my own space.

How long have you been here?

She pauses, a tulip in one hand, scissors in the other. Three years? Yes, that's right, I bought it three years ago. Oh, that makes me feel so old.

She was born the same year as his son, and is a householder, a professional, an adult. Tom will never be any of these things. He tries not to think about this. She is looking at him, those big, grave eyes set in a rounded face.

We can talk about him, you know, she says, but only if you want to. I won't mention him, unless you want me to.

He is moved, enough to touch her hand as it sits on the tulips. Maybe later, he says.

So they do not talk about it during the meal. She has roasted plaice, with tomatoes and herbs and lemon. She thought this would be a good combination, and she is relieved to find she is correct. They sit, facing each other at her tiny fold-out table in the living room. She tried and then rejected a candle on the table, for being too romantic, and compromised on side lights. The room is dimly, but evenly lit. They work their way through the bottle of wine, matching each other glass for glass. He becomes more wry. She becomes more open.

He learns she edits textbooks for a living, she reads, she swims. She likes to go out to the waterfront and look over to the docks in the distance.

She learns he is a company director, his daughter is an engineer, he plays a lot of tennis. He is dreading retirement. He has experimented, unsuccessfully, with hair dye.

Of course, it was Anna's idea, he says. One of her many ideas.

Oh dear, she says, caught between a laugh and a swallow of wine.

I looked ridiculous. Like a particularly grizzled badger. And older than ever.

Will it really be so bad? she says. Retirement, I mean. Think of all that time to do things.

That depends, he says, on if you want the time to do things.

You could find new things. Nice things, to do with Anna?

I'm not sure Anna would particularly want that, he says.

But, she starts, and then is unsure how to go on.

He sits up a little straighter. Oh, she has her own life, her own routines now. The last thing she wants is her old husband cramping her style.

She looks at him then, this contained, reassuring, trim shape of a man at her table, with his salty hair and gentle tilt to his chin. I'm sure that's not true, she says.

Nothing's the same, you know. Not as it was before. He shakes his head. But I suppose I can always use the time to catch up on my reading.

He is suddenly grey and smaller again, and she cannot bear it. I remember, she says, every night on that holiday, it was always you who read to us before bed.

He seems delighted. You remember that?

Oh yes, she says. My mother never read to me. It was wonderful to have that.

Do you still write? he asks. You used to make up all those stories. You and …

Me and Tom, yes, she says steadily. She meets his eyes. Tom was his son and he is gone, she thinks, in a rush of alcohol and confidence. He deserves to know. She speaks again, quickly, to get the words out before she loses the bravery to say them. The thing is, we didn't exactly make them up, you know.

I'm sorry, he says, I don't quite understand.

I want to tell you this, she says, but I'm not sure you'll get it. But I feel I should, at least, try to explain.

Try me. He is very still. His wine glass is empty.

Imagine, then, she says, imagine you could leave here right now, and go somewhere else.

He frowns. Is this a hint?

If you are mocking me, she says, I won't tell you. I can't.

I'm not mocking you, he says, not at all. Please go on.

It's hard, she says, it's very hard for me to explain, and I've never tried before – you have to know that. I've lived with it, all these years, without being able to say it to anybody. So if I get it wrong it's not because I don't want you to know. I'm not hiding anything. But it's difficult.

Look, Clare, he says. Whatever it is, if it's about Tom, you have to tell me. I need to know.

You'll think I'm mad, she says. *I* half-think I'm mad.

I won't, he says. Start again. And I won't say a word, I promise. This is your story.

Carefully, he looks away, lifts his fork, and starts to rearrange the remnants of the meal on his plate. She relaxes slightly.

Imagine then, she says, out of the corner of your eye, a flicker of something else.

He slides the last grey flakes of fish from the bones.

*

1995

They were going on a Proper Holiday. Clare didn't know exactly what a Proper Holiday was, only that it was a good thing. It was what other people did, and that was why it was good.

They were going with other people, and that, her mother Josie assured her, was a good thing too, although Clare was not so sure. These other people were friends of her mother's. They had two children whom she saw at school but would never speak to. Tom was in the other Year 5 class, their rivals, and Harriet, Harriet was in Year 7, another world – or the Senior School, which was near enough the same thing.

But it would be Proper, it would be good, it would be

right. They would fly over the sea on a plane to an island called Guernsey, and go to the beach every day and stay in a cottage with pots of flowers outside the door. Josie bought Clare a plastic spade, a yellow bucket with ducks on the side. Clare sat in the living room pretending to pile sand from the carpet into the bucket and tipping it out again on to a beach between the flowery outcrops of the sofa and the cold green lino of the sea lapping at her feet.

Josie had also bought herself a bright blue bikini, the first Clare had ever seen her wear. 'What do you think, bug?' her mother said. She stood in front of the long mirror on the wardrobe door, tilting her head, turning to examine the sharp curve of her hip, placing a protective hand over the vaguely unsatisfactory rise of her stomach. Clare was not sure she liked this mother, with her swaying hips, her breasts pushed up in blue ruching. The woman who lifted her arms above her head, and ran her hands through her rough, dark hair and pouted at her mirror was a stranger. And then the reflection smiled, and sighed, and dropped her arms, and it was Josie again, Josie with her tired shoulders and wry mouth, and hands that came nervously to meet each other as if they didn't know what else to do. Clare thought about saying something, and then did not. Josie sighed again. 'Perhaps not, eh?' she said, 'perhaps not.' But she packed it anyway.

'I can't believe you've never gone on a plane,' Mary Anderson said in the playground. 'We go at least once every year. To Tenerife.' Mary Anderson's mother braided her hair every day. She wore forbidden black patent sandals to school and had the best skipping elastic in the class, the green neon kind that never snapped. Sometimes she let Clare play.

'We go to Yorkshire in the holidays, to my nan's,' Clare

said. 'My mum likes it.' This wasn't strictly true. Josie always prepared for the trip with her white-grey look, which would not entirely leave her face until they'd stepped back off the train and were in a taxi, heading back to their flat. 'Well,' Josie would say, stroking Clare's head, 'at least she feeds you up, bug. And you enjoy it, don't you?' It would have been easier for Clare to enjoy the cakes and the ramshackle garden and the cats stretched along the back of the sofa, ready to be petted, without her mother there, but she did not say so. She was good at not saying things.

There were many things she did not say to Mary Anderson now. Instead, she threw the pebble handed to her, and neatly hopped away down the numbered board painted on the tarmac. By the time she returned, picking up the pebble on her way, Mary had lost interest. It was a small relief.

Clare did not say things, but she did write them down. She started by writing down what she would have said, if she was somebody else. Then she wrote down who she would be, if she was somebody else. And then she started writing about the places she would be, if she was somebody else. The Places took her away on dull Saturday afternoons and black school nights, and did not wholly give her back during the days.

She hid notebooks away in her own secret ones in the flat. Certain corners had a dark quietness about them that made them, not less easy to see, but less easy to *notice*. She knew Josie would never think to look in them, that her eyes would just flick over them without realising what they held. And somehow, she knew that anyone else would behave in exactly the same way. My Places, she called them. My Places. And she held them to her as closely as she held her notebooks.

She packed her best notebook for the Proper Holiday.

It was an Easter gift from her nan, a beautiful lined and padded hardback, bound in bright striped cloth. It smelt of cotton and dust, and ever so slightly of fish. 'That'll be the glue,' Josie said, turning it over with her matter-of-fact sharpness. 'It's awfully nice, Ma. You shouldn't have, really.'

'Give it back to the child,' Nan said. 'Goodness knows she'll need it, all those stories she keeps writing. When are you going to show us some of them, eh?'

'I can't,' Clare said. And then she felt bad. 'Not yet.' She was pleased with this comment. It suggested that one day she would be able to let them see something, without ever committing to a date or a place. At the same time though, it seemed somehow wrong that she should be given a blank book and expected to show the giver what she wrote on those pages. When I grow up, she thought, I'll buy both the paper and pens and then my words will belong to me alone. Like the Places.

Josie sighed again when she saw the notebook sitting there in the suitcase, atop a tangle of T-shirts and swimsuits. 'You'll have far too much to do, you know, to be writing your stories all the time. We'll be at the beach and out seeing things, and you'll have Tom and Harriet to play with.'

'They won't play with me,' Clare said.

'They will as well,' her mother said. 'And I'd like you to make the effort with them, please. They're nice.'

'Why couldn't we go away on our own?' Clare asked. 'Just you and me.'

'Clare, please,' Josie said. She sat down heavily on the side of the bed, and pulled Clare to her, with her long, tired arms. 'Won't it be nice to have some other people to play with? You and me on our own, well, we're on our own together such a lot. That wouldn't really be a proper holiday, would it?' She drew Clare closer between her knees, pressed her lips against Clare's forehead in one of her hard, dry kisses. 'It'll be fun, bug,' she said, close to Clare's eyes. 'I promise.'

That night, Clare wrote about a wood, about dark, twisted trees that spiralled up to the sky and she was small and white and pale beneath them. There were pools of water that were perfectly round and blue, that glimmered and vanished as she turned to look at them. The trees bent down towards her where she stood and whispered something she couldn't quite hear. She waited for them to speak again.

And then her mother's footsteps came down the corridor. 'Clare, turn that light *off*!' She snapped the book shut, and slid it into the Place behind the bedstead.

When Clare awoke the next morning, it was clear Josie had already been up for some time. A chilly cup of tea sat on the side, and her mother was dressed, her suitcase placed neatly in the middle of the lino, close to the door. It was as if Josie couldn't wait to be away from here. She was drying dishes with a brisk abandon, while the radio chattered away behind her. The last of the juice and milk had been left out on the table, along with a mottled brown banana. 'Eat up,' Josie said. 'They'll be here in an hour.'

They were Anna and Marcus, and Harriet and Tom, and a dull grey taxi and driver. He tossed their battered suitcases into the boot on top of Anna and Marcus's smart black ones, and then Josie took Clare round to the sliding door at the side.

'Hello girls!' said Anna. 'Ready for your holiday, Clare?' Marcus turned to smile at them from the front seat.

'Clare, why don't you go in the back with the kids?' Josie said, pushing the seat forward so that she could crawl in.

Clare would have rather stayed next to Josie, sandwiched between her mother's jeans and Anna's floral dress, but she did not know how to say it. It was easier to climb through and fit herself into the gap next to Tom.

'Say hi to Clare,' Anna called from in front, as the driver slid the door shut and the engine started. Clare looked to Harriet first. Gingery strands of hair flopped over the sides of her face so that Clare could not see her eyes, and two black wires snaked out from under the hair to the tape player in her hand. Tom turned to her. 'I see you in the playground,' he said, 'don't I? You're friends with Mary Anderson and that lot.'

'Sort of,' Clare said. 'Only sometimes.'

Tom dropped his eyes again, and nodded, as if he understood. 'I don't like them very much,' he said.

'Me neither,' Clare said.

They were silent the rest of the way to the airport. In front of them, Anna made Josie laugh in a way that Clare never could.

Marcus paid the taxi driver. Josie tried to intervene, but Anna laid a hand on her arm. 'We'll sort it out later, Jos.' Josie was not a Jos, had never been a Jos, but today she was. And Jos laughed and smiled and told Anna in a strangely light voice that they most certainly would. Marcus and Anna and Josie/Jos piled the suitcases on to a trolley, which Marcus wheeled over the road and into the airport building, trailed by Harriet and Tom. The women and Clare followed behind, Anna extending her arms out to her children to steer them like the dainty china shepherdess on Nan's mantelpiece.

Clare stayed small and quiet and still in the airport. She was not sure about the big, flat, grey corridors and the brown carpets that seemed to roll on forever between glassy walls. She sat next to Josie on the hard plastic seats, bags piled at their feet, while Marcus and Anna took the other two off to the newsagents to buy magazines and chocolate.

'Are you nervous, bug?' Josie said. 'About the flying?' It was the first time they'd been alone together since getting in the taxi that morning.

'I'm not sure,' said Clare. Since she'd climbed into that car this morning, everything had felt a little off-balance, as if the world was tipping sideways.

'It'll be all right,' her mother said, 'once we're up.'

Anna had insisted Clare have a window seat, as it was her first time, so when they took off, Clare watched the runways and fields and buildings rushing by, until with a little drop and pitch, they were rushing away from her instead. The seats shook and rumbled to the sound of the engines, and the fields in her little plastic porthole were suddenly lost in cloud. They could be anywhere, in this noisy row of seats in the white mist. Josie squeezed her hand. 'We're up. We're flying.'

Clare sucked hard on the lemon sweet the stewardess had handed to her earlier. Flying was not how she'd imagined it to be. But then, very little was.

2

The Lone Isles

I saw Marcus Chilcott last week, she tells her mother.

Marcus Chilcott? Her mother's voice is sharp and tinny in the phone receiver, close to her ear.

We were shopping in town, she says. Well, not we. I was out shopping. And he was out shopping. Separately.

But you hate shopping, her mother says.

I still have to do it, don't I? she says. I still need to buy things, occasionally, like everybody else.

Like everybody else, her mother says, and laughs. Oh bug, but you've never been like everybody else.

So they do not talk any more about Marcus Chilcott. They do not talk about the meal at her flat that ended, after the stories had been told, in a soft, dim-lit silence and a long moment where they ended up with their arms around each other, before he left for his hotel. They do not talk about the series of texts sitting on her phone, which is a small dialogue about how nice it was to see each other, and how they must do it again soon, and then how soon, and where.

And they do not talk about how, that night, she got up from her bed and sat for a while at the top of the stairs in the dark, feeling her way into each muffled, carpeted crack of the steps. Just to make sure, she tells herself. It is just to make sure.

She is used to not talking. As a child, she did not talk, and as an adult who lives alone, she is out of practice at it. She can easily spend a day in her flat shifting plates and clothes and discarded tissues from room to room without needing any words to move them. She sails on the silence in daylight, when it is the silence of running water and passing cars and the occasional hum of a fridge. This is a clear, adult silence, in which she is competent and more confident than she ever is with words. She catches sight of herself occasionally in this quietness, in a mirror or a window. The reflection is perfect; a woman, paused, calm, expected.

But the night silence is different. It pulls away at everything around her. It reaches out from the soft darkness of the corners behind bookshelves, and the cracks in the window frame, and that tiny glass square above the front door. She knows it, and yet somehow, it does not know her. She can press her hand into those corners where the sound and light vanish, and yet somehow her hand still remains whole and here. I can't believe, she thinks, that I was ever able to do this. That I was ever able to break through. She sees Tom's face, with that bright smile pinned across it, as he turns to look at her, as he climbs in.

In the mirror, she is only shadows and half-imagined gleams.

Marcus Chilcott acts as if he believes her. This is nice of him, she decides, considering he has very little proof with which to make a decision. But Marcus Chilcott is nice generally. She has been learning this, over the course of a blustery Saturday, when they walk out over the hills outside town and end up with the last two seats in a little slopey-roofed pub.

He is a quiet man too, something she had not remembered. It is fine while they are moving, and their dialogue is punctuated naturally by forks in the path and a slippy, precarious stile, but sitting still and steady in the pub, she realises it is Anna who is the talker, Anna who takes hold of Marcus's silences and transforms them. She tries to catch some of Marcus's pauses and make them into her own, but it does not work. She panics.

I mean, she says, that is, you could say, it is, well — and he places a hand on her shoulder.

It's fine just to sit here, he says, really.

So sometimes, in between the talking, they just sit there. She settles into the distance between them, the quietness that suggests it divides them, the quietness that is bringing them closer.

When they do talk, it is sometimes about the things she has told him. She is careful to preface anything she says with the line: Remember, it was a long time ago. This may not mean — have meant — the same thing to Tom.

And she always still stammers over that past tense.

I know, he says. Really, I do.

And it doesn't change anything, she says. If it is real, I don't know how to get back. I don't even think anyone could get back.

I know that too, he says, but tell me anyway. Tell me everything. Either way, I like to remember.

All right, she says, emboldened by the seaglass green in his eyes as they examine her from behind his spectacles. She leans forward into the silence.

*

1995

The Guernsey cottage had three bedrooms. Marcus and Anna would have the biggest room upstairs, Tom and Harriet a long dark chamber leading off the kitchen with bunk beds, and Clare would share the other neat, piney twin upstairs with Josie.

After Josie had carried their suitcases in with the help of Marcus, she went over to the window and rested her elbows on the sill. 'Well, that certainly beats the High Street for a view, eh?' she said to Clare.

Clare tucked herself in, under her mother's arm, and they looked out together, down a little sloping lawn to a rangy line of trees. 'See, in between them,' her mother said, 'that little gleam? That's the sea.'

'How big is this island?' Clare wanted to know, and Josie couldn't tell her.

'We'll ask Marcus later,' she promised her. 'Marcus will know. But they're not that big. You saw the islands, when we flew in, remember?'

Clare had seen them. A tight bunch of dark green dots nestled in shining blue, which became bigger and the distance between them further until the green was suddenly the flat hard ground coming up to meet them as they landed.

'They seem a long way away from home,' she said.

Josie laughed. 'Not far enough for me.' She pulled Clare closer. 'Home's only an hour's plane ride away. It'll all still be waiting for us, when we go back. And I'll bet you won't want to go back either, not after these two weeks.'

Anna and Josie went off to the supermarket in the hired car, a big Volvo with a funny pop-out seat in the boot.

'Tom'll sit there,' Anna said. 'He's the only one of you who's small enough.' He was much shorter than Clare, with a tiny frame that seemed to show the shape of every bone through his translucent skin. When they had sat together in the airport, Clare had marvelled silently at the tiny width of his wrist against her own.

Harriet, on the other hand, was all rounded flesh, splashed with gingery specks and freckles. When she sat, her thighs pressed out from her denim shorts, and under her printed T-shirt, Clare could see the ridged, threatening outline of a bra. She had not spoken much to Clare since they arrived. She had, in fact, not spoken much at all, but vanished soon after their arrival to lie on the bottom bunk in the gloom and listen to her Walkman.

'Do go and say something to her, Marcus,' Anna had said, before she and Josie left. 'I've warned her about this sort of behaviour already.'

Marcus had placed a hand on her shoulder and nodded. But, as far as Clare could see, he had not left the sunny living room, where he had been sitting with Clare and Tom, poring over the leaflets in the wicker basket on the sideboard.

When the women had driven off, in a flurry of maps and directions and lists of picnic food, she had felt odd at first, left alone in this bright, empty house without Josie. But Marcus had invited her to help decide what they were going to do in such a gentle way that she felt perfectly at ease here, leaning back against the sofa, her toes brushing the square of sunlight from the French windows.

Together, they looked at the fold-out map, on which the island became a big green triangle, edged with half-moons of bright yellow beaches. 'It's up to you two to pick our first beach for tomorrow,' Marcus said.

'Really? What about Harri?' Tom asked, kneeling up over the coffee table to get a better view of the map.

'Harri could too, if she was here,' Marcus said. 'But she's off doing other things. It's your call.'

All the beaches had names that were a little strange and yet familiar – Havelot, Fermaine, Vazon. 'It's almost French,' Marcus told them. 'We're actually nearer to France than England here. All the places are a mix of both.' Rocquaine, Pembroke, Fontanelle. They stumbled over some of the names and Marcus helped them, repeating them until they all ran together in a beating, humming rhythm. Moulin Huet, Cobo, Belle Greve.

'Belle Greve and Moulin Huet,' Marcus said, and 'Belle Greve, Belle Greve, Belle Greve, Moulin Huet.' The chants went on until Clare dissolved in helpless laughter between the sofa cushions.

'It's like magic,' she said. 'They sound like magic.'

'They will be,' Marcus promised. 'You wait until we get there. Magic.' He stood up. 'I better see what Harri's up to. You two let me know now.'

Tom looked up at her, from where he sat on the floor. 'They probably are, you know. Some of them.'

Clare did not quite know what to say. She looked back into his dark eyes, which provided their own shade, even here.

'Petit Port,' Tom said, 'that's where we'll start. Petit Port.'

The words rang with a slightly different rhythm when he said them. 'Petit Port,' Clare said, trying to copy it, 'Petit Port.'

Tom smiled at her. In the sunshine, his skin was so white that it seemed to glow.

They had soup that first night, tomato soup and cheese and big long crusty loaves of bread. On the way back from the supermarket, the loaves had split out of their paper bag, and rolled loose around the back seat of the car, covering the cushions with rough crumbles of crust. 'Ruined,' Anna said, 'ruined.' She threw up her hands

'Don't worry,' Marcus said, 'we're about to cover those seats in sand anyway. It'll only get worse.'

'Exactly,' Anna said, gesturing at the open door of the car. Her bracelets clashed on her wrist. 'Who knows what's been on these seats?'

Behind her, Josie shifted from hip to hip. 'Oh, I'm sure it'll be fine,' she said, but Anna didn't seem to hear her. She had turned to face Marcus. 'I'm not sure we should eat them now really. Particularly not the kids.'

'It'll be fine,' Marcus said, 'honestly, darling. It'll be fine.'

'Think of the germs,' Anna said.

Josie hesitated. 'Let's carry them in, at least.' She laid a hand on Clare's shoulder. 'Come on, bug, give me a hand.'

Clare followed her mother back to the house, with a carrier bag in each hand. As they climbed the slate steps to the door, Clare could still hear Anna's voice, high and clear down on the gravel drive. 'Maybe we could pick the crust off?'

Marcus's reply was lost in the slam of the car door.

So they all had soup that first night, and cheese. But Anna did not eat the bread. She watched, from one end of the long kitchen table, as they all took piece after piece from the wooden board, her wine glass gripped in one hand, and her soup spoon in the other. She only interjected once, as Harriet reached for her fifth slice. 'Shut up, Mum,' her daughter said, and Marcus jumped in, to start a different conversation with Josie.

'Lord knows,' Josie said later, when the two of them were alone in their room, 'what all that fuss was about.'

Clare was lying in bed, watching her mother brush her hair before she returned downstairs to join the others. 'It was the germs, wasn't it?' she said.

Josie put the brush down and came over to sit on Clare's bed, her weight pulling the sheets over Clare's legs with a comforting tightness. 'Perhaps.' She dipped down and gave Clare her brusque kiss. 'Sleep well. And don't write tonight. We'll be up bright and early tomorrow and I want you fresh for it.'

Clare did not write that night. She fell asleep and dreamt of Tom, and being sucked into darkness by the whirlpools of his eyes.

Anna was singing the next morning as she set out plates on the table. She sat Clare and Tom and Harriet down for breakfast and officiated over orange juice and tea and the distribution of cereal from Variety Packs. Meanwhile, Josie and Marcus packed mats and spades and buckets into every corner of the car.

It was a short drive to Petit Port, which was just as well. The day was already hot, and Clare was pressed in the middle of the back seat, between the crook of Josie's arm and the curve of Harriet's leg. Harriet had the window open, with her face turned away into the breeze and her headphones in her ears. Clare leant into her mother's ribs and listened as Anna and her mother shouted to each other over the headrest.

When they pulled up in a small car park, Clare couldn't see the beach at first. A high furze of gorse bushes skirted the clearing, and above them, sky. The adults lifted the bags out of the boot and then they all set off down the small path towards the cliff's edge. Once they had cleared the gorse, they came out on to a small ledge. Below, a steep set of steps on to a wide curve of golden sand. In front of them a clear and steady line of blue, glittering sea.

'Oh lovely,' Josie said. 'Lovely, lovely, lovely.'

She turned to smile at Clare. It was a smile that held no trace of the tiredness that usually hovered at the edges of her face. Clare grinned back. The breeze caught at the shorts round her legs.

Climbing down took a long time. The steps were uneven, with only a single metal handrail. Clare kept her hand firmly on the rail and her eyes on her mother, clambering down below with Marcus. Every so often, they would have to stop to wait for Anna and Harriet, who were talking to each other in raised voices at the end of the procession. Marcus carried a battered white polystyrene surfboard under his arm, which bobbed back and forth as he descended, and wobbled in the wind when he and Josie paused to wait for the rest of the party.

When they were all finally down, they struck out across the flat, free expanse of sand. Under their feet, it began soft and sugary and then became smooth and compact. 'The water line,' Marcus told her. 'That's where the tide comes up. Every day, the tide comes in and makes it all new again.'

'I like that,' Clare said.

'Me too,' said Marcus. 'Come on then, tell me, where should we make camp?'

They settled on a sheltered stretch of sand in a rocky corner, towards the corner of the cove. The adults and Harriet laid out mats and towels and settled down, with sunglasses and books and Harriet's ever-present Walkman. They had all stripped off their outer clothes and were wearing their swimsuits. Josie had braved the blue bikini, but Clare thought it looked too bright and brash against Anna's black halterneck one, and she knew Josie did too.

'Why don't you and Tom go and explore?' Anna said.

'Oh, well,' Clare began. She didn't know if Tom did want to go and explore. And even if he did, she didn't know that he wanted to do it in her company. He was so strange and silent, she couldn't even begin to guess what he wanted, not really.

To her surprise, Tom spoke up. 'All right,' he said, in his flat voice. 'Let's go.'

'Don't go out of sight,' Anna said. 'And lunch in an hour.'

Josie only glanced up briefly from her magazine. 'Have fun, bug.'

They started walking. Tom set an urgent pace and Clare kept up with him, because she did not know what else to do. 'Look,' she said, 'if you don't want me here, I can go off on my own. I don't mind.'

His dark head whipped round to look at her. 'Ssh,' he hissed. He paused, as if listening for something. 'Come on,' he said then, and began to run, with his bandy legs striking hard and fast against the sand. Clare followed him, her breath bouncing in her chest.

He was running towards the side of the cliff as if he knew what he was looking for. And then Clare saw what he was running towards and knew it too, a dark crack between two slabs, wide enough for a child to slip through.

Just before they reached it, Tom stopped, and she stumbled to a halt beside him, panting. He took her hand, sticky with sun cream and sweat. 'Look,' he said, 'look at that.'

Clare looked at the split in the rock in front of them. The jagged edges quivered and bulged towards them. 'Tom,' she tried to say, but the word swelled and stuck in her throat.

'You can see them, can't you?' Tom said. 'The cracks?'

Clare thought of her Places, the small, trembling dark corners of the flat at home into which she slid her notebooks, how safe and small and far away they were. 'I didn't know,' she managed. 'I didn't know they could be as big as this.'

'It's all right.' Tom said. 'Really, it is. I promise.'

And then they stepped forward, hand in hand, and the darkness folded wonderfully on top of them.

3

The Wild Wood

When I think of that summer, he says, out of the silence, it's always the two of you I see. You and Tom. Skipping away over the sand.

They are at the seafront, resting their elbows on the battered rail of the promenade, looking out towards the docks. It is a bright spring day, one of the first of the year. The sunshine warms their backs, the wind chills their faces. Down below them, on a swathe of sand leading to the water, a couple of children attack the ground with spades.

They were good days – at the beginning, she says. Lovely days. I'd never really been on holiday before, you know.

I remember that. He turns to smile. Your face on that plane. Eyes so wide I thought they'd fall out of your head.

She meets his gaze and smiles back. A cargo ship slides by.

You know, she says, I never quite knew how it came about. That holiday. Mum just announced it, out of the blue. And I never thought to ask her why. Isn't that odd?

He shrugs that off. At that age, I suppose you don't, he says. But it seemed all quite simple, really, at the time. Anna and Josie, they were friendly, then, and I think that, well, Anna, she and your mum felt you should have a summer away. For both of you, really. And we were looking at cottages in Guernsey anyway, so it was easy enough to get one that was big enough for us all. And I—

Go on, she says.

He braces himself against the rail and rests his chin on his folded arms, staring down at the sand below. And I, well, I suppose I thought it might be good for Tom to spend some time with someone else his age. To make a few more friends.

She nods. I see.

Tom, he wasn't good at making friends. I wanted to help.

Neither was I, she says. It's not the only thing that matters.

No, but maybe it would have changed what happened. Maybe it—

We can't know that, she says. Maybe nothing would have changed what happened.

He is still staring fixedly down at the sand. I'm sorry to go on, he says, it's just I haven't talked about this with anyone for a very long time. Anna, she went to counselling, you know. She tried to make me go too, but it didn't do any good. It's nice to talk to somebody who was actually there. Who knew Tom.

Talk as much as you like, she says. I don't mind at all.

And it is the truth.

He reaches over to cover her hand with his own. You are very good, he says, to indulge an old man like this.

For the second time, she meets his eyes, green and frosted over with memory. Not old at all, she says.

He gives her another gentle smile. In some ways, he says, I feel like it was you who knew Tom best out of all of us.

It is her birthday the week after. She can't remember if she did mention it to him or not that day on the promenade, but when she gets home from some quiet drinks with a couple of work friends, there is a card from him on the doormat, and shortly afterwards her downstairs neighbour comes up with a full, red and pink bunch of flowers that had been delivered earlier in the day.

The message on the flowers is simple, written in a florist's round, innocuous hand. *Dear Clare, happy birthday and thank you. Marcus.* But the flowers themselves are brilliant, bright blooms, clustered together noisily in a profusion of ribbons and fronds.

Dead posh, Lilian-from-downstairs says approvingly, as she hands them over. You're a lucky girl.

He's just a friend, she says, and can feel a warm glow begin at the base of her jaw. Really, nothing but a friend. A good one.

Oh aye, Lilian says, laughing. Well, I'd stay friendly with that one, if I were you.

Lilian winks and shuffles back down the stairs, and she retreats, with the conspicuous flowers held close to her chest. Inside, she finds a vase and places them on the side table. She tries to carry on with her evening tasks as usual, but her eye keeps being drawn back to the loud splash of colour.

Later, she catches herself stopping, between bathroom and bedroom, to press a petal lightly, tenderly, between her fingers.

In the end, she rings him, the next lunchtime, from a bench outside the office. Thank you for the flowers, she says. They are lovely. You shouldn't have.

Oh, it was my pleasure, he says. He sounds fuzzy and far away.

You really shouldn't have, she says, again.

I wanted to get you something, he says, to– His voice furs into static.

I can't hear you, she says.

Sorry, he says. Is this better? Can you— He recedes away again into a long hiss.

Never mind, she says, never mind. Let's try again some other time. She waits for a reply, but none comes.

She ends the call and sits there for a moment afterwards, wrapping her coat tighter around her. Everything feels cold and grey and downcast. She realises, after a moment, that this feeling is disappointment.

Dinner, then? I owe you a proper dinner.

It is eleven days after her birthday, ten since they last spoke. She has not even had to count back to check this is correct. He is back in town that evening and at a loose end.

A last-minute thing, he says. Plans changed, he says. Completely unexpected.

He says.

She has thrown out the wilted flowers only that morning.

It would be easy to be busy, she thinks. Very easy to choose a reason not to go. She toys with the idea of turning him down. It would be safer that way.

And it could, she supposes, be all in her head alone. What proof has she to go on, a dinner in exchange for one already given, a press of the hand on a seafront, a bunch of faded blooms at the bottom of a bin? Any friend could claim as much. She knew his son once, a son who is no longer here. Is that not enough for him to acknowledge her as a friend?

Go on, he says, let me take you to dinner. I can't promise it'll be as lovely as the meal you cooked for me, but I'd like to return the favour.

So yes, a favour, once given, and now returned. That is all this is.

I don't know, she says.

Oh come on, Clare. Call it a belated birthday dinner, if you must.

But what about the flowers? she says.

He laughs, and the sound bounces down the phone line. Meet you at the station, seven thirty? Does that work for you?

He does not laugh often, now. How does she know this about the older, newer him already?

They meet directly beneath the big old station clock, completely by chance. She has run from the bus stop, pulling out her phone to check where he will be. As she hurries into the station, she looks up and sees a lean, greying man, glasses pulled down low on his nose, suit jacket slightly creased from a day on the back of a desk chair, striding across the concourse. He has not seen her yet. She allows herself to watch him as a stranger, as a man she has never met before.

There are a thousand of them here, these middle-aged men, tracing lines they walk every day through this station, with briefcases and rucksacks. They follow their trails to work and then home again, each to a house and a wife and two ebullient children. She walks through them every morning on a trail of her own, never stopping to consider any of them further than this.

She has always assumed the man she will love will not be one of them, that he is out there somewhere beyond these well-trodden tracks. He will only be transformed into one of these creatures by time and the swell of her abdomen. And she will continue to love him in spite of it, because he is *her* creature, and he has been formed by their life together.

But this man walking towards her, this one of many, is a man she believes she could come to love. He is already firmly walking the tracks of a life that he has not built with her. And yet, he catches sight of her, and with a pleasing directness, turns quickly towards her. She feels her heart tighten, in the same way as it used to back then. It is pain and longing and thrill all in one quick pulse, and she cannot stop the smile from coming to her face.

Right on time, he says in greeting, gesturing to the heavy black hands sailing around the face above them.

For this, she thinks, maybe she has come too late.

It is a lovely meal, despite his dire warnings. He has chosen well. They sit opposite each other, carefully negotiating a wine list and a shared dessert menu. They order coffee, to make the meal last just that little bit longer – on her part, at least.

They walk back towards the station together. His hotel is just around the corner. They are walking slightly too close together, and occasionally, their shoulders bump against each other. She is not sure, now, who is walking towards whom.

Well, he says, isn't this where you turn off?

Yes, she says, this is me.

They stand, facing each other on the corner of the street. He sighs.

I have to confess, Clare, I thought about not coming today, he says. About not seeing you again.

She feels that thrill pull through her chest. So did I, she says.

But we had a wonderful evening, didn't we? It was truly lovely to see you. But I don't want to – I think, maybe we shouldn't do it again. You're so ...

He swallows. She watches the long, angular movement of the bone and muscle in his throat, and has to fight the desire to touch it. But still, the certainty of knowing that he would welcome that is enough.

Oh god. This is just too dangerous for me, Clare, he says.

There is still time for her to escape, back to the life she expects. He will let her go. He is a good man, after all.

Walk me home, she says.

It is not a question.

Later on, inside, when it finally comes to it, when she finds his lips on hers, his tongue seeking her own, it actually feels surprisingly simple, as if their bodies were always meant to fit so cleanly together, his arm slotted over her shoulder, her pelvis tight against his thigh.

Don't let me, he says, please, Clare, don't let me.

She lets him.

*

1995

She could remember very little clearly after that first moment in the cave, other than the beat of her heart in her chest and the pulse of Tom's hand in her own, the two matching each other in a strange, desperate movement. She did not sense so much as *know* that they had at once half a foothold on that beach and half a foothold in somewhere else, quite separate from both the people and the place they had left behind. The chill of the sand trembled under her feet, and the damp, salty rocks seemed to shift and reform, and as she stared at the clumps of mussels and weed in the gloom, they bulged and exploded into light and colour and clear, joyful sound. And at the centre of this was Tom, the boy, the leader, walking her on, talking the brightness into being, holding her close with one hand while he reached out with the other through air that rippled a euphoric petrol spill of colour at his touch.

And then they turned back and out through the jagged gap of hard, definite sunlight, and they were standing on a beach again on the same summer holiday day, facing a blue and white parasol and a bending orange windbreak.

'I told you,' Tom said. He dropped Clare's hand.

She could not speak. She stepped back and away from Tom, to lean against the rocks, pressing her palms deep into the sharpness of barnacles and salt. Even though the day was sunny, the sand and the sky seemed suddenly grey and flat. She watched a woman on a striped towel grab a small boy by the arm and rub sun cream in mechanical, circular motions over his back.

'Are you all right?' Tom asked her.

She managed to nod. She did not know how to put it into words, not yet, not so soon afterwards.

'You'll get used to it,' Tom said, 'you'll see. It's all right, you know. We'll go further, we'll go right the way in, next time.'

He shifted from one foot to the other, and then stood a little taller, and grinned, suddenly triumphant. 'That's the first time,' he said, 'the first time I've ever taken anyone else with me.' Into his pale cheeks came a proud blot of colour.

Back at the rocks, Anna and Josie lay neatly, side by side, eyes closed, pressed up into the sun. Harriet had set herself a little way apart, turned away on her side and curled protectively around her Walkman. They were so eerie and still, on this bright beach, that they seemed locked in time. Had everything just stopped for them while she had been so, so far away?

She walked slowly towards them, following in the sandy prints of Tom's feet. What should they do to wake them? She thought about Sleeping Beauty, lying asleep while the tendrils of the forest climbed around her, waiting for a prince to rescue her. In her mind, she saw the tide rise, and the dark sea reach up around them to claim them, washing into Anna's light hair, between Harriet's curled knees, over Josie's tight, neat face. They could not let that happen.

She turned to Tom, aghast, but could not find the words to tell him.

And then Marcus was coming nearer and nearer, sea-water beading on his skin, the surfboard gleaming under his arm, shaking drops from his dark head like a joyful puppy. 'The water,' he said, as he caught up with them, 'the water is wonderful! Fancy a dip?'

His words breathed a slow life into the figures on the sand. Anna stretched her hands above her head, Harriet unfurled herself crossly and rolled over, and Josie, Josie sat up and looked into the sunlight.

'Mum!' Clare said. She left Tom's side and came to kneel on Josie's towel.

'What's up with you?' Josie said, squinting at her.

Clare looked at her mother, alive and awake and wholly present beside her. She wanted to tell Josie how relieved she was, how she wanted Josie to always be beside her, just like this.

'You'll stay here, won't you, Mum?' she said eventually. 'You won't go off anywhere?'

'You're a funny one, aren't you?' Josie lifted her hand and tucked a stray strand of Clare's hair behind her ear. 'Don't worry, I'm not moving from this towel.' She raised her gaze to Marcus. 'And I definitely won't be going anywhere near that awful cold sea.' She lowered herself down on to her back. 'Why don't you go have a paddle though?'

'You too, Tom,' Anna said. She looked down the length of her body to find her son. Tom stood and looked back at her, in silence. He had not moved since Marcus arrived.

'Come on, guys, I'll take you, if you like,' Marcus said. 'Harriet, are you coming?'

The Walkman was pulled off one ear for a second. 'I don't bloody think so.'

'Language, Harriet!' Anna said, but she spoke upwards, to the blue sky, and the words fell away into the light and the wind.

'Come on,' Marcus said again, and he tapped Clare on one shoulder, and Tom on the other. 'I'll bring the board with us too.'

As they started to walk away, Clare heard a voice behind them. 'Clare!'

She turned around. 'What?'

Josie had raised herself up on her elbows, and was looking earnestly at her. 'Remember, don't go out of your depth. Promise me you won't.'

And Clare promised. She could do nothing else.

It felt oddly exhilarating, to turn her back on the people and the rocks and that dark cave crack beyond and walk down towards the water, a flat, dark blue line stretching on and away into the distance. 'Let's run,' said Tom, and she knew he felt it too.

He set off, in the same urgent, focused way he had this morning, and Clare began to speed up too. Marcus, keeping pace easily with his son, caught hold of her hand, and she was carried along by the thrill and the speed of the hand in hers. As they got nearer the waterline, their feet began to smack harder and wetter against the ground, and she laughed in delight, the sound jolting up and down in her throat.

She did not normally run in this way, not even in the playground. The only times she ran this fast were when she and Josie saw the bus coming round their corner and were too far away to make the stop in time. And even then, she was usually weighed down with bags and coats and the apprehension of missing the bus, which always made her late for school, and Josie cross with herself for being 'a rubbish mum'.

'You may be a rubbish mum,' Clare said to her once, 'but you're still my mum, and you're my one and only mum.' It was meant to sound comforting, but didn't quite come out like that. It made Josie cry, which she only did occasionally, and Clare was even less sure about how to handle that.

But no, this running, which made her feel light and free and fast, was a world away from buses and bags and tears, and all those other pieces of her life that didn't quite seem to fit here. So she laughed, and above her, Marcus laughed too.

Marcus did not stop at the water's edge, but carried on running, pulling her forward into the splash of the waves. She shrieked at the chill crashing up and around her legs. He came to a stop when they were ankle-deep, and let the surfboard down on a strap to bob between them.

'You'll get used to the cold,' he said. 'It's fine once you're in.'

Around them were other children and parents, tentatively testing the waves, and further in, clusters of gleaming shoulders and heads, moving in time with the swell of the shining darkness around them. She looked for Tom. He was standing a little apart from them, knee-deep, looking out towards the skyline.

'Up you get, then.' It was Marcus. He patted the surfboard.

'Me?' Clare said.

'Yes, you first.' Tom turned around to look at them. 'I'll take you next, Tom. Ladies first and all that. Swim with us, though?'

Tom waded towards them, and waited as Marcus helped her lie flat on her stomach on the board, hands gripping the sides, legs trailing off the end. The water was cold against her chest and legs, but Marcus was right, she got used to it, and the sun felt warm on her back. Marcus kept a firm hold of the strap on the front of the board.

'Ready?' and Clare nodded into the battered polystyrene. 'Hold tight then,' he said, and took off running deeper into the water, strap in hand, pulling Clare behind him.

She shrieked once, in surprise, and then let herself feel the rush and flow of the water past her clutching knuckles and out between her dragging toes. She closed her eyes against the splashes Marcus was making as he ran ahead of her, and held on as she felt him slowing, and the weight of the water expand and deepen under her.

'Clare!' She opened her eyes to find Marcus and Tom's heads at eye level in front of her, Marcus with his feet steadied on the invisible seabed, Tom bobbing up and down in the waves.

Tom was grinning at her, in the same way he had that morning after the cave, and in that instant, she knew why. It was here too, pockets of that mysterious, trembling, wonderful darkness, somewhere deep beneath her floating body.

'What do you think, then,' Marcus said, 'of swimming in the sea?'

She grinned back, and below her, felt another world flicker and dance in and out of being.

'It's amazing,' she said. She touched her tongue to her lips and tasted the sharp happiness of salt.

It seemed to take forever to climb back up the cliff that evening. By the time they left the beach, the rocks had started to stretch a long, grey shadow over the towels and the bags and the white surfboard, propped up to dry. Josie gave Clare a rough dry T-shirt and shorts to put back on over her swimsuit. Her skin was damp and salt-sticky, and she felt sand slide between her toes in her sandals.

'Did you ever see so many steps?' Anna exclaimed, pausing halfway up the cliff face, at a little strip of a stopping place just wide enough to hold a bench.

'I'm definitely not coming back here tomorrow,' Harriet said behind her. 'You can forget that idea right now.' She had red patches marking the freckle of her arms, and the bridge of her nose was tinted pink.

'We're almost there, Harri!' Marcus called back. He and Josie were ahead again, Tom and Clare scrambling in their wake.

'Such a stupid place to come,' Harriet said, loud enough to be heard, but Marcus chose not to hear her.

Marcus and Josie stopped to let Clare and Tom catch up. Anna and Harriet were far behind, the tops of their heads crawling up the flights of steps below. 'Are you all right?' Josie asked Clare.

Clare nodded. Her legs were tired, but inside her mind was a bright, clear wakefulness. She had so many things she wanted to go away to her room and think about, and things she wanted to ask Tom without Harriet or the grown-ups overhearing. They had spent the rest of the day mostly with Marcus, swimming in the sea and building towers in the sand, and perched in a row on the wet surfboard in the sand, eating sandwiches. There had been no chance to talk to Tom again about what they had done that morning, and while they were with Marcus, he had seemed to avoid venturing too near to the cave again.

Perhaps she and Tom could find a way to be alone properly, later on. She watched the pale backs of his legs lift and fall on the steps above her, following them steadily on and up.

As they neared the top of the cliff, a man was there, standing at the very top of the steps, looking out to sea. He was a short, squat figure, wearing an old green padded jacket that didn't quite close at the front, and with a long, grey ponytail of hair tied low at the nape of his neck. He was smoking a cigarette. The solid streams of smoke curled away in front of him and then disappeared into the breeze over the edge of the cliff.

'Hi there,' Marcus said, 'beautiful evening, isn't it?'

'It is that,' the man said, 'it is that indeed.'

He did not turn away from the sea to look at Marcus, or Josie. But when Tom came past, he glanced down at him with sudden and earnest attention and did not look away again.

Tom started, then bent his head and walked quickly on. As Clare came past after him, she felt suddenly chilled – as if all the brightness had been leached from her skin. She caught up with Tom just as they reached the car park.

'Did you know him?' Clare said.

'No,' Tom said. 'But I didn't want to talk to him.'

Clare couldn't think of any other questions to ask. They stood there without speaking, waiting for Marcus to unlock the car, and their T-shirts shivered in the breeze.

'Here you go, bug.' Josie passed her a jumper. 'Give me

that bag, and then jump in the back with Tom while we wait for the others.'

She climbed in after Tom, and Marcus shut the door with a click behind them. The sounds of the breeze and the birds and Josie's voice all melted into one distant murmur. She pressed the warm, comforting wool of the jumper close to her chest. From the car window, she could still see the head and shoulders of the man on the cliff, looming above the yellow gorse.

They sat together in the soft plate-glass silence, waiting.

4

The Hidden People

So, about this magic then, he says.

What about it? she says.

They are lying as they have lain every morning this week, close and still together in the sheets of her bed. He likes to pull the top sheet up over their heads and lie there in the cottony gloom, noses pressed together. Watching his eyes open and close, eyelashes flickering in and out of focus, she wonders, is this something that all lovers do? She has no frame of reference for a man in her house, in her bedroom, in her bed, other than this one here. This is Marcus, with his tough bones and breathy exhales, who leaves short, salty grey hairs on her pillows and basin, and pulls her body into unfamiliar shapes in his embrace. It is a situation that is entirely new, and yet now she cannot imagine what life was like before it.

With their heads together like this they whisper, even though there are no housemates to overhear their conversation, no neighbours with an ear to the floorboards. This togetherness is their secret, a secret so great that they have not yet even discussed it between themselves. But they let their skin and muscle and bone converse at will – his hand to the curve of her thigh, her cheek to the sharp nub of his collarbone, the lock of her legs around his hips. And when the chatter of their bodies finally dies down to a low murmur, they let their limbs rest against each other and whisper under the sheets.

Is it here, in this room? he asks.

She shakes her head. The sheet rustles and dips in front of her face. No, there's nothing in here. Not now, anyway.

He pushes it away, lifting the sheet and pressing his palm to her cheek. How can you tell?

They change, all the time. Or they used to, anyway. I couldn't tell you why.

And you could feel where they were? You and Tom, you could both feel the same ones exactly?

We could, she says. Or that's what it seemed like, anyway. At the time.

It all seems so strange, he says.

I told you, she says, you don't have to believe me. You can think I'm mad.

You are many things, but you are very definitely not mad. His thumb circles her lip, once, twice, and comes to a stop in the very corner of her mouth. And I want to believe you. Or, at the very least, I don't want *not* to believe you.

And it's so blurry now, she says. When I think of it. Of them. Like looking the wrong way through binoculars. It's been so long.

Since – Tom?

She nods, bringing her hand on top of his, and feeling her own cheekbone through the lattice of his fingers.

But you still know where they are? When they are?

She considers this, rolling away from his hand, his body, to lie on her back and look up into the closely patterned weave. Sometimes, she says, into the fabric, and the words sit there, trapped on her lips. I feel them sometimes. Or at least I think I do. Which is probably much the same thing.

He pulls the sheet away from her face and sits up, placing his hand on her hip. She blinks and looks up at him, this strange creature in her bed with mottled skin and that strong slope to his shoulders, who reaches towards her in chill morning light and does not wait for her to reach back. She has no word for him. He is not a boyfriend, he is not a partner, he is not even a one-night stand. She does not know what he is.

There's a place, she says, at the top of the stairs, where the corners in the step seem darker.

He has already lifted himself up and on to her. The dark cracks shiver and contract at his touch.

Of course, both of them still have daily lives that must continue to run on some sort of course, even if it is a slightly less firm one than before. Her dark and quiet nights are now invaded by this movement, this heat, this fervour, and as a consequence, her days become less concrete, less crisp around the edges. She finds herself in the mornings on the muggy jumble of the train with very little memory of how she got there, and still conscious of his touch on her lips, her thighs. She looks around at the other people standing in the carriage, tinged grubby yellow in the underground light, and wonders how many of them still have a partner's hand on their skin from the night before. Together, they all rush through tunnels and stations, and they steady themselves against handrails and partitions.

And he, Marcus has a life that should have been whole before – a life with a solid wooden frame, that feels steady and warm to the touch. This is the life he goes back to, when he leaves her each time, this is the life that he takes his bag and coat towards every other evening when he is not here with her. She sometimes looks at his big tweed coat, spread over hers on the hook, and wonders about the other places that it hangs. Does it sit over one of Anna's jackets, one of Harriet's scarves, as tenderly as it embraces her own? She cannot know, and she tries hard not to think about it.

When the speckled tweedy coat is not on that hook, she misses it, with a sharp, fierce breathlessness that takes her by surprise. But it is also a relief, to look at the neat red collar and sleeves of a coat so clearly and familiarly her own, and see it relax into the space that surrounds it.

They talk about his framed picture life at some point, in those first few weeks. She starts the conversation, perhaps because it feels as if they have been avoiding it since the very first evening in her kitchen. She notices it pressing on her lips every time she moves to kiss him, and it is uncomfortable to have it sitting there.

What about Anna? she says, one night, after they have washed the dishes, but before they switch out the lights. It comes out a little louder than she means it to, and it startles them both.

Anna? he says, rolling the name over and around his teeth. Anna.

I mean, she says, where does she think you are, all these nights away? Does she really think you're at some hotel?

This is not what she means at all. She means, do you think about her? Do you tell her you love her? Do you go home to her and press your nose to hers under the sheets?

I have a lot of business trips, he says, I always have. Perhaps never so many, so close together before, but I have them.

Doesn't she think … anything?

I don't know what she thinks, he says, abruptly. It doesn't matter.

Oh, but it does, she says. It does to me.

Really, can't you just forget about her for now? Please, Clare, please.

She is unsure what he is asking, why he is asking it. I can't, is all she says. Marcus, she's your wife. The two of you are still together.

We're not together, he says. He has become very hard, as if all his bones have compressed themselves into small, sharp angles.

She tries not to sound frightened when she says Marcus, I don't understand. Don't you live with her?

Jesus, Clare. Can't you, of all people, you with all your *magic*, understand that it's not that simple?

She looks down at her fingers, gripping the back of a chair with tight, white intensity. She thinks, this is how it ends, then, in my kitchen, just like it began. She thinks, I lived so many years before him. I can live after him.

He takes a deep breath, and moves away to look into the frosted window, lifting a hand and steepling his fingers against the wavy pane. I'm sorry, he says. Look, we've not been close for years. Ever since Tom, really. It was like we couldn't find the words to talk to each other any more.

Yes? she says

I can't really explain it. Like on that day, remember that day on the cliffs?

He turns back, seeking her nod, and then sighs.

Silly question. Of course you do, of course. Like on that day she was standing on one cliff, looking down and instead of standing right next to her holding her hand, I was on another cliff, too far away to even shout. So far away, and I have been ever since. It's like a … gap. He bunches the tea towel in his hand.

She comes up behind him, and slips one arm around the tight points of his ribs. A crack, she says. He softens.

Together, they stand here, pressed into each other. People pass by the streetlight outside, making dark flickers in the glass.

He is, as is so often the case, right. It is not that simple. None of this is.

Come out Wednesday after next, her friend Meena says over coffee that Saturday.

Wednesday is a night that he often works away from home. So it is often a night that his coat hangs on the hook behind the door. But she will not know this for certain until her phone sings with a text, just as she unwraps her sandwich at her desk.

Wednesday's a bit difficult for me, she says. Can we make it Thursday?

Then she remembers he does sometimes come on Thursday instead. But not as often as he comes on Wednesday.

Actually, no, hang on, she says, Friday?

Oh, sorry, no, I'm going away that night, Meena says. We have to go see Rich's parents for the weekend. It's his dad's sixty-fifth. It'll be horrific. I'm going to have to meet all the relatives. Like, *all* of them. You know, a big family thing.

Meena rolls her eyes, and she feels compelled to mimic the gesture, although no, she does not know. She does not know at all. There are her events with him, and then there are his events with his family. The two can never coincide. This is the best option. For a second, she allows herself to imagine walking into a Chilcott family garden party, a faceless pair of octogenarians in cane chairs and a raft of squabbling siblings and cousins passing out cake. And Harriet, of course. Harriet would have to be there too.

She does not even know if his parents are still alive.

So you definitely can't do Wednesday or Thursday, then? Meena is saying.

I— she says, and takes a quick sip of coffee to give herself time to think. She has not mentioned him to any of her friends, and she does not want to have to start to explain now, over cups full of grainy dregs and foam. And anyway, she is not sure she can.

He may not come on Wednesday. And if he doesn't, he will come on Thursday.

She sets the cup steadily down in its saucer. I think Thursday I could do, she says. Yes, let's say then.

She lets herself think that she can always cancel, after all.

She is a woman who used to rely on a schedule, who balanced out her days and nights between sociality and solitude, who measured out the time of her life in careful, elegant portions. He has upset her scales, and she is unsure how to right them again, or even if it is possible.

Do you have any brothers or sisters? she asks.

He has come on Wednesday, arriving at her flat with a laptop bag, a pizza and a bunch of lilies.

They sit together on the sofa, his arm around her and her feet tucked up under her hips. She is pleased to see him, and is relieved that he has come tonight and not tomorrow, but she also feels herself become irritable with his arrival.

He wrangles a slice of pizza from the box. Two sisters, he says. Georgie and Ellen.

Older or younger?

Georgie's three years older, Ellen's a year younger.

And do they have children? she says.

Georgie's got a couple of boys, and Ellen has just one little girl. Well, not-so-little girl any more, I suppose.

It is unusual for her to ask so many questions, all in a row. She makes herself force them out. Do you see them often?

He rests the pizza slice back on the cardboard and his hand becomes firmer on her shoulder. Hey, my darling, what is this?

I don't know anything about your family, she says, that's all.

Oh, there's no need. They're all terribly boring – but well-meaning – people, he says. We have nothing in common. Harriet's the only one of them that really matters to me.

Still, she says, I'd like to know. And your parents, too. I want to know about your parents. Even if – even if they know nothing about me.

He takes off his glasses and rubs his eyes with his hands. He is suddenly both older and younger, all at the same time.

This isn't easy for me either, he says. I hope you know I would love nothing better than to be able to introduce my parents to you. Well, I mean, my father's in a home now and can't even remember his own name half the time, let alone mine, but still, I'd love to be able to at least give it a try.

She looks away, down at her neat, contained knees, recognising the sincerity in his voice.

But my darling, beautiful Clare, he says, reaching forward and lifting her chin. The thing is, even with all this, you make me so, so happy. I haven't been so happy in a very long time.

He kisses her and she feels her arms reach up around him

of their own accord, as if a spell has been cast on her body that she cannot find the incantation to undo.

That night, for one surprising, joyful moment, she trembles right on the edge of that black, otherworld euphoria, as if a Place has opened up inside her own skin into which she can disappear, just as she used to do. And then the deceptive shiver fades, and she is back in his arms, with his weight heavy and earthy on top of her. It is not enough.

*

1995

'We mustn't let anyone else know, you know.'

This was the first thing Tom said to her the next morning, as if he had been thinking about it all night. The words came out faster than usual, as if he knew that they hadn't got much time before they would be interrupted. They were sitting in the living room together before breakfast, listening to the grown-ups fussing in the kitchen. Harriet was still asleep, and Josie and the others were talking so loudly next door about shopping lists that there was no way they could overhear them. Tom sat high on the sofa, and Clare on the floor beside it, kicking her heels against the rough pile of the carpet.

'I know,' Clare said. 'I haven't told anyone.'

'Nobody? Even before?' Tom said.

Once, despite her misgivings, Clare had tried to explain to Josie, when she was very young. Josie had stared at her, a smile hovering around the corners of her lips. 'That imagination of yours does beat all,' she had said eventually, and stroked Clare's hair, with the slow softness that meant she was thinking about something quite different to the thing they were talking about.

'Nobody,' she said, 'nobody at all.'

'Well, that's good, then,' Tom said, 'at least.'

She didn't need to ask him why not. There was a secret feeling around each Place – a sort of dark, silent privacy that did not welcome outsiders. They did not want to be known about.

'Have you ever told?' she said.

Tom shrugged, bringing his feet up on to the sofa and crossing them under himself, so he looked like the small, solemn sultan from her book of the Arabian Nights.

'I think it's only kids who can find them, you know. I used to think Harri might be able to, so I told her. But she couldn't. And then she told Mum, who wanted to send me to a doctor. But Dad said to her not to. People think you're crazy.'

'It's weird,' Clare said, thinking. 'I never met anyone else who knew what they were. But mine are different. Mine are smaller.'

'Some are,' Tom said. 'I used to think they were only small, too. But then we were on the beach one day last year, and I found that one we went into yesterday, just by accident, by walking past, really. You know, how when you get close to them, you can feel where they are?'

She nodded, and thought again about the strange, trembling excitement of finding one.

'There's lots of them all over, here,' Tom said. 'I don't know why. Even some in properly weird places like under the water, too. I used to have a map, where I marked where they were. But I can't find it now. I must have left it behind last summer.'

'Oh, but we can make a new map,' Clare said.

Cross-legged on his throne, Tom smiled. 'I knew you'd be able to see them, that first time I saw you. When you meet someone else who can, you just *know*.' Then he bent down, and came close to Clare's ear. 'But remember, we have to do it secretly. Nobody else can know. Nobody.'

Then Anna came into the room, in a clash of bracelets and perfume, and he sat back quickly against the cushions. They were out of time.

It was fun that morning, sneaking about under the gaze of Josie and Marcus and Anna. Clare knew she was sneaking much more than she needed to, but it was good, for once, to have a secret that she could share with somebody else. She retrieved her best notebook and pen from under her pillow while Josie was in the bathroom, and she and Tom slipped out into the garden together.

'You going outside?' Marcus said, seeing them come out into the hall. 'Take a jumper, Tom, or you'll have your mum on your back. The sun's gone in and there's a bit of a breeze picking up.'

While Tom fumbled about on the coat rack, Clare slid a map of the island out from the pile of leaflets on the sideboard, unnoticed. She presented it triumphantly to Tom when they reached the safety of the back terrace.

'There,' she said, 'now we can make the map again.'

The garden was a long, thin, rambling strip of lawn that wandered down from a top terrace to a clump of tall trees clustered together at the very bottom. It was hemmed in by white-grey stone walls, and a dark, narrow wooden shed set under the trees.

The garden itself was very exciting, if only because Clare had never before lived, even for two weeks, in a house with a garden of her own. Their flat at home had a small concrete yard shared between the occupants of the block, which somebody in 10a had tried to brighten up with a couple of tubs of flowers, but the people had moved out, the flowers had bloomed and died, and the tubs now sat in the corners, collecting water and cigarette butts. Her nan's house also had a garden which she was free to play in when they visited, but Nan herself had a tendency to come out with Clare and watch her to make sure she didn't tread on any of the flower beds, which wasn't quite the same.

However, this garden here was still not exciting enough to contain a Place. They trod the lawn up and down, skirting the walls and the trees, and pulling at the big lock on the shed door, crusted over with rust, in an effort to sense any slight tremble that might suggest one existed.

'Nothing there,' said Tom, and he and Clare returned to the terrace, to sit on the bench and consider.

Clare unfolded the map and looked again at the small yellow slivers of beach. The names were more familiar to her now, after that first day. 'Can you remember where you found them last time? We could go there.'

Tom peered at the paper. 'There's one at Vazon Bay. I think.'

'Well, let's ask your dad to go to that one next,' Clare suggested. 'Maybe even today.'

Tom looked up at her, his eyes dark. 'I heard Mum promising Harri we'd do something else today. She thinks beaches are boring.'

'Oh.' Clare was disappointed. 'Well, maybe tomorrow.'

'Harri thinks *everything* is boring,' Tom went on. 'Dad says it's just her age, and I'll understand when I'm that old. But I never want to be like that.'

'Me neither,' said Clare.

They sat for a moment and watched the leaves of the trees

jostle each other in the wind. And then Marcus stepped out on the terrace. 'Hey, kids, come in for a second? You have to come and see this.'

In the hallway, Anna and Josie had their heads close together over a big, blue plastic tub, by the open front door. Harriet was leaning on the sideboard behind them, arms folded. There was a new smell in the room, a fresh, hard, fishy odour. 'My god,' Anna was saying, 'they're so big. Look at those claws!'

'Claws are all bound,' a new, strangely familiar, voice said. 'You'll get no nips from them now.'

Josie and Anna's heads parted, and between their profiles Clare saw the short, ponytailed man from the cliff, holding the tub. Beside her, Tom flinched.

'Clare, Tom,' Marcus said, 'this is Jem, our neighbour. Do you remember, we saw him coming back from the beach yesterday? He catches crabs and he thought we might like some for our tea.'

'Come and look, bug,' Josie said. 'I bet you've never seen one of these alive before.' She held out an arm, and Clare sidled under it, suddenly glad of its comfort. From the safety of her mother's embrace, she regarded the contents of the tub. A heap of brown, gleaming crabs lay inside, their shells speckled with green, and the hard, curved pincers of their claws taped closed with red bands. A few waved their bound claws up and down, or swivelled their solid, bulbous eyes to look around the curved, scratched walls of the tub.

She dared to look up at Jem. Close up, he had a fleshy, red-tinged face, big, firm eyebrows, and some straggling grey hairs for a beard. He was still wearing the green jacket. 'They're something to look at, right?'

Clare felt the same chill shudder its way down her spine.

She shrugged, and turned her face away into Josie's ribs.

'Oh come on,' Josie said, 'don't go all shy on me now.' Clare pressed closer into her, and Josie sighed.

Jem chuckled, a deep swoop of a laugh with a sharp edge. Tom edged further back towards the stairs.

'Thanks, Jem. We'll take five,' Marcus said. 'You'll all have some, right, kids?'

'Yuck,' said Harriet. 'I am so not eating that.'

Marcus shook his head, in mock despair. 'All right,' he said, 'let's say four.'

Anna found a washing-up bowl from the kitchen, and Jem carefully hooked four glistening creatures from the tub and dropped them into the plastic box.

'What will we do with them until dinnertime?' Anna said, eyeing the crabs with nervous suspicion.

Jem chuckled again. 'Most people pop them in the bathtub.' He looked down at Clare, still tucked into the crook of Josie's arm, seeking out her eyes. 'Don't worry, little miss. They'll never escape from there.'

'I feel slightly bad for eating these fellows,' Marcus said, looking down at the four crabs edging their way around the slippery sides of the bath, 'but they will make an extremely tasty tea. There's nothing like fresh crab! You two will give it a try, right, even if Harri won't?'

Clare nodded. Tom stared silently into the bath.

'That's my girl,' Marcus said. 'I hope Tom here will follow your fine example. I better go down and check we have all the things I'll need to cook them.' He left the room, whistling as he descended the stairs.

'I think that man knows,' said Tom. 'About the cracks.'

Clare stared at him. 'How can he? And anyway, he's so old. Older than your dad, even.'

Tom twisted the tap of the basin, back and forth, back and forth. 'I don't know,' he said. 'But I'm pretty sure he does. I can just tell.'

They stood over the bath, looking at each other. Below them, the legs of the trapped crabs scrabbled against the enamel.

5

The Ghostly Voices

Once, he says, there was a tower.

A tower?

With a princess living inside it.

Trapped there, I suppose, she says. Like they all are.

Ah, no, he says. This one was different. This one could have got out and come down to the town any time she liked. She just preferred not to.

The alarm starts to pipe its morning song. Sensible girl, she says. She reaches over to the side table to silence it, and picks up her hairbrush.

He takes it from her hand with authority and starts to pull it through her hair.

That's not the end of the story, you know, he says.

She sits and marvels that she can let him do this without snatching the brush back, turning her head away, getting up and leaving the room, pulling the door shut behind her. I know, she says.

He brushes steadily, cautiously, pausing at every catch of bristle on strand. Her scalp tingles.

They both have stories to tell that the other one has never heard. It is a treasury of mutual family detail, illustrated in rich anecdotes – he said, she said – and bound up in memory. They listen to each other's tales carefully, considerately.

Did you know there's a grave? he says. Even though there's no body in it. Everyone thought it was important. To have one.

Everyone?

He shrugs. People. Anna. My sisters. For us. For Harriet. Something to do with the grieving process.

There was a funeral, she says. I remember. I didn't go. I don't think I even realised it was going to happen until the day.

A pale Josie, seeing her on to the bus on her first day of term, paler than ever in a borrowed black suit jacket, buttoned too tightly at the waist.

Anna didn't want Harriet there either, he says. But she was insistent.

She thinks of teenage Harriet, of her sulky, freckle-splashed indignation. I can imagine.

I was glad to have her go, he says, if it helped her. I'm not sure it is a help, really.

It didn't help you?

He sighs, sits back. I don't know. I can't remember a lot about it. There were so many people there, and I had to talk to all of them. That's what I remember the most. The incessant talking. All the people want to talk to you. And you … the last thing you want to do is talk.

I'm sure they meant well, she says.

Oh god, of course they did! That's the worst part.

He reaches for her hand and she lets it slide into his, pressing her fingertips against his knuckles with a firmness she hopes is reassuring.

Anyway, he continues, the grave is there. In that giant

cemetery on the city road. I don't visit it much, although Anna does still, I think. I don't think Tom would care, either way.

She offers him the start of a smile, and he squeezes her hand close. He's not there, really, though, is he? he says. He never went to that place even when he was alive – you know where I mean, that horrible, square patch of land by the A-road covered in stones and wilting flowers in polystyrene holders. He's still out there, somewhere. Wherever that somewhere is.

You can always remember him, she says, even if you don't know where he is.

She lets herself see the dark head of the boy, the firm eyebrows, the intense lines of the mouth, the thrill in the eyes. She wonders if these are the same things that Marcus or Anna see when they think of their son. Or whether, as their memories recede further away from the real person and they all grow older, Tom starts to become somebody quite different for each of them.

I do, he says. Every day.

I think of him a lot too. She rests her other hand on his arm.

That's comforting, somehow, he says. That even after I'm gone, there's someone else who will carry on remembering.

I hope to be around an extra few years, at any rate, she says. Although I'm not promising anything. The gods don't like it when you try and drive too hard a bargain.

He laughs, and she is pleased she has managed to draw this reaction from him. He leans over and kisses her temple. She files this moment, this sound, this kiss of affection, not of want, away in a dark corner of her memory, where it will give off its own soft glow.

He holds her to him. My darling, he says. My love.

She folds her forehead to his shoulder, and his arms move around her as if he is trying to press her right through his bones into his chest. Their ribcages swell, crashing against and into each other. She thinks of the foam on a dark sea.

Of course, he says, close to her ear. It's not really a grave, is it, though? It's called something different. You know, when there's really nothing under there at all.

Another night visit comes around, just like all the other ones that have preceded it. He arrives when the sky has already become dark, and sits on his side of the sofa, and she on hers. Even though really, it is all hers, most of the time. She tries not to think this.

We should go on holiday, he says.

Holiday? Where?

I don't know. Just … away. It would be nice to be away. Wouldn't you like a holiday?

I would, but, she says. She thinks about the idea of sitting next to Marcus on a plane, in a taxi, of walking next to him on a beach. Of sleeping, and waking next to him, and then that next night sleeping again, on and on, in the same bed, as if it was the normal way they lived their lives. The vision makes her giddy, breathless, in a way she can't quite vocalise. But, she says.

Just a short trip, he says. A few nights. And don't worry. It'll be my treat.

I can pay, she says. Honestly, I don't mind. But. She stops again.

Hey, he says. If it's not the money, then what is it?

I don't know, she tells him. This relationship – this he says, she says story of their own – seems to belong so entirely within the walls of this flat that it is hard to imagine it breaking out of these boundaries and continuing to take place outside of it. Even for just a short trip. A few nights.

Look, we don't have to, he says. If you don't like the idea, that's fine. I just thought it would be nice for us, that's all.

He turns his head away from her again, and looks into the brightness of the television. A woman in a red jersey informs them about high-pressure fronts sweeping into the area. She watches his profile flicker in the blue light – his long, dipped nose, the droop of the side of his lip, so familiar now.

It would be, she says. I'm sorry. You're right. If you'd like to go, I would too.

He looks back towards her and smiles. Great. I'll look up some options. I promise we'll have fun, he says. Just us, together, doing things. It'll be lovely.

All the things they might do together. All the meals they might eat, the people they might talk to, the places they might go and sit with each other and look together at views, at buildings, at events. This is what people do, she reminds herself. This is what we all do. Do you remember, they might say to each other, months, years, later. Do you remember when?

People need stories. People need stories that are theirs to share.

Later, she tries to share a story that is not Tom's, but entirely her own. She is sitting on the side of the bed, roughing her wet hair in a towel, one foot dangling over the edge. He is moving about the room, taking off his shirt, fetching a glass of water, folding his clothes over a chair ready for the morning, with the methodical certainty that he applies to everything. The room is softly dark, lit from the pool of light around the one lamp on her side of the bed. She never expected to need a second one.

I've never done this before, you know, she says. Not really.

This?

Been with someone properly. I mean, for a long time. Longer than a few weeks.

He stops and looks at her, trousers hooked over his arm. Is that a problem?

No, she says, no. It just means it's all a bit strange for me, that's all. All this stuff like, well, holidays.

He comes to sit next to her. Look, if you don't want to go, I can understand.

No, she says, I want to. It's just going to take some getting used to, that's all.

He cups her chin in his palm and brushes the wet strands of hair away from her cheek. They cling damply to the back of his hand, and he makes no attempt to remove them.

It makes sense for him to be here, she knows this. They have to meet here, all the time, because there is nowhere else. So it must be here. All the time.

I haven't lived, she says, her voice rising against the warmth of his hand, I haven't lived with anyone in ever so long. I'm not sure I know how to do it. Especially not like this.

You're doing just fine, he says. Honestly. Just fine.

He kisses her, and the reason she can kiss him back and roll away into his embrace tonight, and all that follows after, is because she can let herself think of the night after this one, and perhaps even after that. Nights where she will curl up alone under a smooth sheet, and feel herself breathe in the scent of her own skin, and turn in her bones, and swim out alone into the darkness on a chilly tide of sleep.

She knows this is not something that can be considered to be just fine. But there is no way to explain this to the man beside her. He has lived most of his life in the same sheets as another person. He has a body that is used to reaching out, halfway through sleep, and finding the warmth of some-body else's skin there, radiating against his own. But her spine and hips and legs will slide unbidden away from him after they start to fall asleep in her bed, pressing up against the edge of the bedframe.

Even after all these nights together, her body still flinches when his hand brushes her back, jolting her back into a close, black wakefulness. She closes her eyes against the dark, and sees the empty bed, the hollow in the centre of the mattress.

On the nights he is not there, as she slips out into sleep, she sometimes misses the possibility of his fingers grazing her spine, the sudden sharpness of a cough, the thrill of an unpredictable turn in the bed beside her. But this strange, quick longing is not enough to make up for the happiness that comes when she twists, and flexes out into the relief of the crisp, empty space.

In the end, she knows she is simply not a strong enough swimmer to take another with her.

*

1995

Clare stood next to Marcus, looking down at the boats in the harbour. The net lifted and spilt its load on to the deck. Fish scattered, and some flipped up and away across the boards. 'They slither,' Marcus said, and she repeated it – took the unfamiliar word out of his mouth and tasted it in her own. It seemed like silver, like the wet slick of the fish against the wood. A silver slither. A slither silver. She leaned a little further out over the rail, nearer to the gleaming and flapping below. He reached down for her hand. 'What are you murmuring to yourself down there?' he said.

'A story,' she said, and then emboldened by the shine, the air, the bright sea smell and the shouts of the gulls, 'a secret. A secret story.'

'I want to know your secret story,' he said.

'No,' and she pulled her hand from his. She dared to look up.

'I want to know your stories,' he said. 'Won't you show some to me?'

She knew he was talking about her best book, the cloth-bound Easter book she kept slipped inside the rough cotton pillowslip of the holiday cottage. The one she liked to write in when they got home at the end of their days out. The one not even Josie was allowed to see.

'Maybe,' she said, relenting. 'Maybe I'll show you. One day.'

Marcus laughed. 'I'll hold you to that, Clare.' He put a hand on her shoulder. 'Come on, let's see where the others have got to.'

Tom was standing outside a shop window on the other side of the road, running his fingers back and forth over the peeling white paint of the frame. It was a clothes shop, with three mannequins leaning at odd angles in the windows, their arms reached towards the street, draped in bright, pat-terned dresses of the sort that Anna liked to wear.

'Hey, buddy,' Marcus said, 'what have you done with the girls?'

Tom nodded glumly in the direction of the doorway. 'They're in there. Looking at stuff. Just looking, they said.'

He turned his big, dark eyes up to his father. 'Can we go somewhere else now?'

'In a bit, Tom.' Tom sighed, and knocked a hard ridge of paint from the wood beneath. Marcus took his son's shoulder and turned Tom around to face him. 'Come now, we've all spent the past few days down at the beach so you and Clare can run around and swim and play. Let them have their time too.'

Clare knew why Tom was frustrated. They had gone to the beach again yesterday – a different beach, a flat open bay, that stretched out in a gold crescent, flanked by boxy white buildings and a tall, regular sea wall. There were no steps to climb down here, no cold, damp caves to explore, no outcrops of rocks covered by bulging, green-dark clumps of seaweed. Just a bright, chattering curve of towels and windbreaks, jumping and billowing in the wind, and clusters of people weaving tracks down and back between the seagrass and the waterline.

'Vazon Bay. This isn't the beach I thought it was,' Tom said, as they stood, ankle-deep in the water, surveying the crowd. Their parents and Harriet were a small cluster of blue and red and yellow in a spread of coloured blots on the open sand. Clare thought about her space book that showed the galaxy of stars in the Milky Way, with an arrow bending round and into the tiniest of insignificant dots somewhere at the edge of the spiral. You Are Here. The tideline of water around her shins suddenly felt chilly, and she hopped forward, out of the wave.

'Look at all these people,' Tom said, a foamy edge of disgust seeping into the last word.

'You never know,' she made herself say, although she was not at all sure herself, 'there might be something hiding, even here. You never know.'

'I know,' Tom said, looking round and away from her, from the stone tower at one end of the beach to the squat group of caravans at the other. 'We won't find anything here today. We'll just have to choose better tomorrow.'

But tomorrow came cloudy, with a chance of rain – or so the television said. Harriet pointed this out to both her parents that night, gesturing triumphantly with the remote. 'See! There's no point going to the stupid beach again then, is there? We can do something else for a change.'

'Well yes,' Marcus said, 'I don't suppose there is, if it's going to rain. Let's find something else to do, shall we, kids?'

Clare glanced over at Tom, who had drawn his feet up to his chest on the sofa and wrapped his arms around them, with a furrowed, crunched-up, willing look on his face, as if he could change the weather forecast by thought alone.

'But we will go back to the beach again sometime, won't we?' she said. 'I'd like to go to some more beaches.'

'I want to go into the town,' Harriet said. 'Mum, you promised.'

'Of course we'll go back to the beach, Clare,' Marcus said. 'Definitely. When the weather's better. But we'll find something else for tomorrow, that's all.'

'It's true, I did promise her, Marc,' Anna says. 'And it'd be nice to show St Peter Port to Josie, wouldn't it?'

From the armchair on the other side of the room, Josie smiled a sleepy, almost-feline smile, running her fingers around the wineglass in her hand.

'Fine,' Marcus said. 'St Peter Port tomorrow it is. And then maybe we can visit somewhere else in the afternoon.'

'Good,' Harriet says, slumping back against the cush-ions, and flicking back and forth through the television channels.

'Oh, for goodness' sake, Harriet,' Anna said irritably,

getting to her feet. She started to gather glasses and cups from the coffee table. Josie stretched and uncurled, getting up to help her.

'Oh leave it, Jos, honestly.'

'No, no,' Josie said. She reached for two glasses, Anna reached for one more cup, and then they were done, moving away into the corridor.

'Just wait until you see St Peter Port,' Anna was saying. 'It's so darling. We're going to have such fun.'

Then the kitchen door swung shut, and all that was left was the mumble of the television. Clare looked back over at Tom. He was still hugging his bony knees together in a tight white grip.

It did not look as if Anna and Josie were actually having such fun, there in the dress shop.

'Clare!' Anna said, when she walked in, leaving Marcus and Tom to wait outside. 'Oh yes, come join the girls. Come here, darling. Your mum's been trying on some clothes. Come here and tell her how pretty she looks.'

Josie was hovering in the entrance to the changing room, in something gauzy and blue, with a big skirt which, on the right woman, would have flowed. On Josie, the skirt hung awkwardly off her angles, the sleeves catching and sagging on her shoulders rather than billowing as they should have done. Would have done, on somebody like Anna. Josie folded her arms, crushing the shimmer of the light material against her chest.

'I tell you, Anna,' Josie said, 'it just doesn't work.'

'Now then,' Anna said, a little too loudly, bringing Clare in front of her, as if to protect herself from the full force of Josie's tense uncertainty, 'tell your mum. Doesn't she look pretty in that?'

Clare moved her weight from one foot to the other. 'She looks different,' she said, carefully.

Behind her, she heard a splutter that was quickly turned to a cough. Harriet, leaning against a wall beside a display of scarves patterned with vivid dots.

'You don't need to pretend,' Josie said. Clare could tell that the attention was making her uncomfortable, and very quickly, cross.

'Oh Josie!' Anna said. 'It is so very much your colour. And the shape is just lovely.'

'She doesn't like it, Mum,' Harriet said. 'Stop trying to force her to like it.'

'Oh Harriet,' Anna said. 'Really, don't be so silly. Honestly, Jos, it's gorgeous. I do think you should have it. I'd buy one myself, only Marc would go mad if I came home with yet *another* one of these.'

Harriet sighed. 'I hate it when you do this,' she said, more to herself and the row of scarves than to anybody else.

'No,' Josie said, abruptly. 'It's just not me. Sorry, Anna.' She backed into the changing room, and tugged the curtain closed.

If Clare had been alone in the shop with her mother, she would have slid behind the curtain with her, and pressed herself into the corner by the mirror, as she always did on shopping trips. She liked to watch Josie dress and undress in such close quarters, noting the thin, square angles of her shoulders, the small low curves of her breasts, the way her waist retreated in and then rolled out again, the hard tapering of her legs to a pair of pointed, surprisingly delicate feet. It was so different to her own body, but the shapes of it were just as familiar, a part of her mother that nobody else knew, nobody else got to see.

But because she was out there with Harriet by the

scarves and Anna standing close behind her, she stayed put, anchored by Anna's hand still resting between her shoulder blades.

'Well now,' Anna said, 'such a shame, don't you think?'

Nobody said anything. Clare looked at the creases of the closed curtain. She thought about Josie inside, wrestling her way out of the cocoon of fine blue threads, emerging with her body intact, taut and hard and recognisable again, with a pool of filmy skirts at her feet.

The day got a little better once they left the shop. Anna came away with a spotted scarf, wrapped in scented tissue and while they waited for her to pay for it, Clare was able to take Josie over the road to show her the fishing boats, now emptied of their loads and tied neatly up in a line at the jetty. Anna wrapped the scarf around her like a shawl, and they all had tea and sandwiches in a cafe near the front, and by the time Anna and Josie had worked their way through the pot of tea, everything seemed almost back to normal again.

'Looks like that rain's on the way,' Marcus said. The first drops were spattering against the small windowpanes behind the net curtains of the teashop.

'It's such a shame,' Anna said, 'for it to rain on our holiday.'

'Let's just go back to the house.' This was Harriet, taking sugar cubes from the little metal dish on the table to balance up into a crystalline, crumbling wall.

'Don't do that, Harriet,' Anna said. 'Other people will want to eat those.'

'*I* want to eat those.' Harriet stopped building for a second to slip one cube into her mouth.

'Stop it now,' Marcus said, in a tone that Clare had not

heard him use before. Harriet raised her hands and pushed back into her chair, with a heavy sigh.

'How about that butterfly farm then?' Josie said, tipping the last of the tea into Anna's cup. 'You like butterflies, don't you, Clare?'

'A butterfly farm?' Clare had never heard of such a thing. 'How do you grow butterflies?' She pictured a field with long rows of plants, butterflies flowering on every stem, ready to be picked off.

'You'll see,' Marcus said. 'That's as good an idea as any, you know. It's indoors.'

'They have a nice gift shop,' Anna said, musing over a sip of tea.

'What do you think, Tom?' Marcus asked.

Tom had been sitting quietly, elbows resting on the table, leaning his face into the crooks of his narrow palms. 'It doesn't really matter to me,' he said, 'what we do today.'

'We'll go back to the beach tomorrow if the weather perks up,' Marcus said, 'I promise.'

And just like that, there was silence. Clare looked around the circle of faces. Their cheeks were slate-grey, sketched by the rainstorm outside. Nobody was looking directly at anybody else. We could be statues, she thought. We might never move again. She sat and imagined the freezing spell taking hold, creeping up her legs into her spine, turning them to granite. She wondered if Tom could feel it too.

'This tea has gone stone cold,' Anna said. 'Let's go.' She set the cup back on the saucer with a loud chink, and just like that, they were all stirring, shifting, breathing flesh again.

The butterfly farm turned out to be a warm, white set of plastic tunnels and rooms, filled with plants in tubs and hundreds of fluttering, coloured butterflies under special strip lights. Rain fell heavy and evenly on the roof, and inside, a fan pumped hot, humid air into the spaces, which made Clare feel she was breathing in water rather than air. Like a mermaid, she thought, swimming through sea butterflies.

They were free to wander inside, through a maze of pathways, around potted trees and structures designed to give the butterflies places to rest, to hide, to breed. There were butterflies here from all around the world, Marcus told them, butterflies they'd never normally be able to see in this country. He pointed out the ones he thought they should know from England too – the cabbage white, the red admiral, the tortoiseshell. Clare did not recognise any of them, except from books. It was not something Josie knew about.

Josie was disconcerted by the butterflies. She kept lifting a hand to bat them away, and then, remembering where she was, dropping her hand again and blinking rather fast. Very soon, she and Anna retreated to one of the tunnels behind a double row of plastic strips, away from the frantic wings and the close, steamy air. Any lingering awkwardness from the dress shop was gone now, as they used their hands to mimic butterfly wings flapping in front of their faces, and lamented the mist of frizz marring their hairstyles.

'I'm fine out here,' Josie said. 'We'll just stay outside a while. Why don't you go on back in with Marcus and look at the butterflies? Go on.'

Clare pushed her way back through the plastic, feeling it fall heavily over her shoulders. She found Tom crouching down next to a big, greenish butterfly on a leaf, with twitching, almost translucent wings.

'That's beautiful,' she said.

'They come in so many different colours,' Tom said. 'It's weird, really.'

Clare looked up and around at the fluttering dots of colour, moving, and settling, and moving again. This was a very different galaxy, here, full of this constantly shifting, flickering life. 'They're like fairies,' she said, without thinking.

She thought Tom might laugh – fairies, so babyish, so girly – but he nodded. 'I think you're right.'

He was so sombre there, dark head hunched over his knees, solemnly regarding the green butterfly, that she felt moved to speak again, feeling the colours playing around her. 'Tom. We still have lots of time, you know. Eleven whole days. We'll find some more of them, I know it.'

Tom raised his head. 'I—' and then he stopped. His eyes moved to her chest. 'Look,' he said, a lot more slowly, 'Clare, look down.'

There, clutching on to the cotton of her T-shirt, wings trembling slightly, was a red, patterned butterfly, with big painted eyes of blue and yellow. It was so close that she could see the fine hairs on the legs, the bright softness of the wings. It was a sea creature, it was a fairy, it was magic. 'Oh,' she said, 'oh.'

'Don't move,' Tom said. 'Don't even breathe.'

She stood still. Over her heart, the butterfly closed and opened its wings.

6

A Timely Escape

They are going to Florence. He has arranged it all. He comes round one evening, and they sit, close together over his laptop, as he scrolls through photographs of richly red beds and gilt-edged basins, and views of terracotta domes against blue skies, and tight, sunlit stone streets.

How about this, he says, or maybe this? What about here? This one is very close to the centre.

I don't mind, she says. Wherever you think best.

She is normally precise in dictating the pattern of her own movements, not usually this passive about her likes and dislikes. But there is something about making a decision in tandem with somebody else that makes her fall silent. She does not want to be responsible for choosing something for another person that may be imperfect, may be wrong, may be disastrous even. It is too much of a risk.

We can go wherever you want, he says. It doesn't have to be any of these places. He tilts the laptop towards her. You can look, go on.

I don't need to look, she says, pushing the laptop back on to his knee. I'm happy for you to choose. Really.

She is worried, then, about seeming unenthusiastic, but he does not even see this as a rebuff. He is intent on the bright stream of images in front of him – bed after bed, building after building. An entryway, clambered over by plaster cherubs. In his mind, she can see they are already there, walking through these streets hand in hand, stopping to eat gelato, returning to these rooms at the end of the day to drop their bags and to take off their shoes, and to shower and to sleep and to have sex. It will not be like this, she thinks – the rooms will seem smaller, the shower might be faulty, the sun might not always hit the streets in quite that way. They will drink too much red wine. They will wake in the morning, restless and hot from sleeping in an unfamiliar bed, disturbed by the clangs and clinks of breakfast being served below. They will not feel like having sex, but they will anyway, because this is what one does, on holiday with one's lover.

The two people who sit here on the sofa are not the same two people who will go on the holiday. Is that a terrible thing to think, to feel, in your bones? She is unsure. She cannot say any of this to him, as he peers at the future he imagines them to have. He selects and clicks.

They meet at the airport for the first flight out. She has taken a taxi, leaving her flat cold and grey and silent in early morning light. As she looks around one last time before descending the stairs, checking over window catches and pot plants and draining boards, she feels a sudden pang of affection for this little place, for each of her chairs and the table and the rows of pictures and crockery, all neatly ranged in the gloom. She misses it, even though she has not yet left it. Then she makes herself close the door on it all, locking it away.

He is waiting at the check-in concourse when she arrives, smartly dressed, with a small, formal black suitcase, in what might pass to an observer as casual business dress. She notices this, calculates, and then tucks the thought away again.

The hall is busy, even at this hour, with people moving in all directions, often following each other in trails, dragging bags and cases over the scuffed shine of the floor. He comes towards her, but his progress is cut off by one of these caravans passing between them – a man, a woman, two lingering, weary children. He stands and waits, and smiles at her over the whir of the wheels.

When they finally come together, they stand facing each other, closer than if they were friends, in the light, in the day, in public. She thinks about whether to kiss, whether to not kiss. He settles it by taking her hand, leaning in and over her.

She feels the solidity of his body, the unmistakable reality of his face against her own. They really are two people, a couple, going on holiday together, to a room with a silk-striped coverlet and outside, streets leading down into a sunlit square. She presses her cheek firmly to the pinstripe of his lapel.

He speaks Italian. Good Italian. This is another thing she does not know about him. She watches him navigate his way through customs and baggage reclaim and the taxi rank with a softly rattling stack of unknown syllables. They tumble out of his mouth as if almost by accident, and she stares at the familiar lips that can form such unfamiliar words. Seated in the taxi, she begins to laugh.

What? he asks. What?

I never knew, she says. That you spoke Italian.

He does not laugh. French and German too, if you want to know, he says.

It is so funny, to her, to be away in another country, with

a man she knows so little, a man who can still surprise her so much. He does not seem to share the joke. He gives her a quick, polite smile, and then turns his head back to look out of the window. Beyond him, the concrete of unknown roads rushes by.

I never knew, she says again. That's all.

How about you, then? he says. What languages do you speak?

I don't speak anything, she says. I don't speak anything at all.

Of course, he has a plan too for their days away. He tells her about it, interjecting odd, relevant, thoughtful details in the back of the cab, as they get nearer the city centre. She thinks, these are the kind of plans he wishes he could make for us while we are at home. He does not like their impromptu, erratic meetings any more than she does. This is his natural tempo too. He carries on.

And then tomorrow, I thought we could start at the Uffizi. There's quite a lot of walking involved, so I thought it would be better to do it after we've had a good night's sleep. You know, while we're fresh. And there's a cafe, on the roof terrace, for coffee after.

He has brought two guidebooks, even though this is a city he has been to before. A long, long time ago, he tells her when they are booking the trip, just after university, and of course, she now realises it would have been with Anna, must have been with Anna. A student Anna, with her sharp lines softened by a youthful roundness in her skin, and the flush of that first thrill of happiness. They had met at university, the two of them, and married three years later. This is one of the few facts she has managed to glean from their nights together.

She does not ask, at the time, why he has chosen to come back here, and it now seems a silly question not to have put to him. But it is too dangerous now, sitting in this car side by side, encircled by leather seats and faint traces of cigarette smoke, to ask it.

There's a restaurant, well, a *trattoria*, really, he says, that's meant to be quite good, just up the street from the hotel. So I booked for tonight. I meant to get there last time, but somehow never quite managed it.

It sounds lovely, she says.

I can always cancel the booking, he says, if you'd prefer to go somewhere else.

No, she says, it will be perfect.

I did check. It still has good reviews, he says, even after all this time.

It will be perfect, she says again. They hold hands, as the car swings round another sharp, unexpected corner.

The plaster cherubs adorn the entry to the hotel, just as promised, but the hotel room itself does not look at all like the one in the photographs. However, it is still a spacious room, if a little gloomy, with a big, high, blue-covered bed in the centre, and a tall wardrobe made from dark wood, with roses etched into the darkness of the doors. He lies back on the side of the bed they have decided, in this particular relationship, will be his, and stares up at the ridges of the ceiling, before closing his eyes against them.

She discovers she cannot be still, in this new resting place. She paces the room out, from wide window to tall wardrobe to the stark, cream box of their bathroom, and then back again. She runs her hand over the glassy top of the dressing table, she pushes the fine film of the curtain aside, she crouches in the bathroom to look in the neat triangle of cupboard under the basin. For the next three days, this is where they will live. She needs to know it.

You're like a cat, he says, from the flatness of the bed. A cat, released into a new pen.

It's a nice room, she says.

Are there any hangers in the wardrobe? he asks. I should really hang up my jacket. He begins to sit up, the striped blue of the bedcover dipping around his weight.

I'll do it, she says. You stay there.

She picks up the suit jacket from the edge of the bed, and shakes it out from the shoulders, smoothing the sleeves. This is new, she has never done this for him before. With the jacket over her arm, she investigates the wardrobe and finds a cluster of wire clothes hangers, nestled together in a corner. There is a dark uncertainty to one of the corners, which she tries to ignore. This is not the time for that, with his jacket pressed against her hip, and his eyes at her back.

Eventually, she manages to detach one hanger from the brood, and slides the shoulders carefully into it. There, she says. She runs her hands down the heavy weave of the jacket one more time, and then hooks it gently, protectively, back into the wardrobe. There.

When she turns back to the bed, she finds he has rolled his head to one side towards her and is regarding her with his clear, steady, green look, broken in two by the line of his glasses.

I wish you could do that every day, he says. This pleases her, with a twist of delight and pride and sadness that she was not expecting to feel.

Me too, she says, and right here, in this moment, it surprises her to discover this is not a lie.

She comes to sit next to him, placing her hand on his leg, and he runs his own hand up, over the spread of her thigh and into her waist. I could do this, she thinks, I could do this, properly. They stay poised like this for a moment, smiling, breathing, hands waiting, hesitant over fabric and skin and muscle.

The sex they start to have then is not in the plan for that afternoon, but yes, all the same it is right, it is correct, it is exactly what they should be doing at this precise moment, in this place, at this time.

They make it to the Uffizi, the next morning, on schedule, hand in hand, her bare arm pressed against his. She is fielding an intense desire for touch, for constant contact, that is new to her. They both slept well last night under the heavy blue waves of cover, he a starfish on his back, she curled in a ball and clutching on to him like a sea anemone. She woke once, to go to the bathroom and then to pause, for one moment, beside that trembling darkness at the back corner of the wardrobe, before his deep, even tides of breath drew her back into the bed. She submerged herself back inside his embrace and gloried in the regular rise and fall of his chest, the scent of his exhalation against her cheek.

As they queue for tickets, in a long, solid line stretching back under arches and along pillars, she keeps hold of one of his hands with both of hers.

Do you want an audio-guide? he asks her. It's a few euros more on top of the ticket price, but do have one if you want one.

I want, she thinks. I want. She wants him, with all the power she can muster in this simple, needing verb, all the time.

I'll be fine, she says. Don't worry.

He puts his arm around her. I can always try and tell you what little I know about it, my darling, I suppose, he says.

I can remember something of the paintings, at least. I'll tell you everything I can.

She takes in these words, quickly, greedily, savouring the imminent prospect of many more.

She had bought a new dress before she left. A summer dress. For any summer, not just an Italian one, she told herself at the time, but really the only place, the only person it fits is here. The neckline sits deceptively high across her chest, before dipping so low across the back that she can feel the seam nudging at the small of her spine. The blades of her shoulders, the nubs of her backbone are suddenly more present, alive to the slightest breeze or the brush of a strand of hair. And when she sits down on a chair, she is instantly aware of the jointed wood pressing up against her bare skin.

She puts it on that night, after the paintings, and the statues, and the walking, and lastly a few hours in the welcoming shade of the hotel room (where they have discovered there is no longer any need for a guidebook at all). She showers first, and by the time he comes out, towel tucked about his waist, she is sitting fully dressed on the bed, pushing green glass stars through the tiny knots of tissue in her ears.

Ready, already?

He seems constantly surprised at how quickly she can organise herself, how soon after deciding to go out she can find a bag, put on a pair of shoes. Anna must take her time.

Don't rush yourself, she says. I'll wait.

You look lovely, he says. Give us a twirl.

She fixes the second fastener behind her earlobe and stands up, smoothing the skirt of the dress down in front of her, and slowly twists the bareness of her back towards him and then away again.

That dress, he says. You look so— He lifts his hand and runs wide tracks through the wetness of his hair.

So?

Just so, well, sexy.

This is not a word he has ever used before. It's not a word she has ever been called before, not by him, not by anyone. It does not feel entirely like a compliment when he says it here, deep inside the blue room, even though it should be.

Beautiful, he says, correcting himself. Beautiful.

She looks down and away. You should get dressed now, she says. We don't want to be late.

It is warm enough for them to eat out on the street in front of the *trattoria*, at a little table with an ashtray perched under one leg to stop it wobbling on the paving stones. It is a perfectly romantic setting, in all the expected ways. There is a red tablecloth, a vase of flowers, a basket of bread chopped into rough cubes, and a proprietorial ginger cat rubbing its way in and out of their legs under the folds of cloth.

Don't feed it, he tells her, it'll only encourage it. But she slips it strips of Parma ham and shreds of mozzarella anyway, enjoying the small defiance.

It's a lovely evening, she says.

There's something very cheering about being able to eat outside, he says, ignoring the cat crouched, nibbling, at their feet. I often think, if we could do this more back home and not just on holiday, everyone would be happier.

We make the most of it though, she says, when we can.

Sandwiches and beer on the beach, he says, that was my favourite. We used to use that old surfboard to sit on, do you remember?

She had put on a cardigan for the walk to the restaurant

but now they are here, among the warmth of the people and the wine and the brush of the cat's tail on her legs, she shrugs it off.

He raises an eyebrow. Are you too hot?

Not at all, she says. I'm just right. A breeze runs up her spine and she shivers at the sensation. He snaps open a piece of bread.

Later, after they have finished the meal and he has paid the bill, they start to walk back to the hotel. He extends an arm and she takes it. With a lope and a hop, he shortens his long strides to match hers, and they fall into an easy rhythm again.

A couple of men, smoking in an open doorway, turn to watch her as she walks past. One of them calls out to her in Italian, something low and casual and playful. She ignores them and smiles up at his profile, expecting to see the start of a smile, a laugh in his cheek, but he is frowning.

Maybe you should put your cardigan on.

Why?

It just might attract less attention, that's all.

She pulls her arm out of the snug corner of his elbow. You really don't like this dress, do you?

He shakes his head. That's not true.

Or, she says, more to the point, you don't like *me* in this dress.

She stands very still and tall and looks at him. His face is shaded from the light in the arches. A motorbike buzzes past and then is gone. The wine and the heat and the low, low back of the dress make her feel potent and reckless and slightly brave.

I told you already, you look beautiful. Just very – different.

And that's a bad thing?

No, he says. No. It's just not something I thought you'd wear, that's all.

She begins to walk again, down the street, away from him. Would you think the same if it were Anna in the dress?

That's not fair, he says, from behind her.

Well, would you, though? I mean, you're married to her.

Look, I'm sorry, he says, running to catch her up. I'm so sorry. I don't know what came over me. The dress is lovely. You are lovely. Just perfect. I just want to take care of you. To protect you. That's all.

She stiffens. I'm not a little girl. I can take care of myself.

I know that, he says.

And after all, I have to be able to, she says, don't I?

Oh Clare, he says, out of breath, my love. Forgive me. Oh Clare. He puts his arms around her. A thousand tiny pin pricks from the creases of his shirt sleeves dance across her shoulders and down her spine, and so she leans in, because she cannot bear to pull away.

On the top of the Duomo the next day, several hundred narrow stone steps up above the city, they stand together and look out over rough-tiled rooftops and towers and pale hills beyond, in warm, holiday sunlight.

So that's Florence then, he says. What do you think?

She is still a little breathless from the climb. It's so different, she manages, so different to anything else I've seen.

He laughs. Catch your breath, my love, he says. Take your time.

My love, he calls her, my darling, my love. In themselves, they are cheap words, said often. She has been called these things many times before, by bus drivers, shambling men on street corners, even Lilian downstairs.

But the words are dressed differently now, with a richer meaning, and she thrills to them in a way she never would have before.

There is nothing more perfect than here, now, to hear this word on his lips. My love. His love. Her love.

My love, she tries out, in her own head, for him. The words fit. She says them again, and this time out loud. My love.

He starts, and then draws her to him. Oh god, I love you, Clare, he says, almost as if he is apologising for it.

She bows her head into his chest, against the fabric of his shirt. This is love, then. This is it. This want, this need, this inexplicable longing to be closer even when you are right up against each other. This is why people do such foolish things, this is how people are undone so completely. There is nothing she can do about this at all.

I love you too, she says, into the tidy point of his shirt pocket.

She feels him kiss the crown of her head, and cradle her closer to him with one arm. They rock together, high above the rooftops. Oh god, he says again.

Eventually, he releases her, and they turn back outwards, still touching, but not looking.

After all, he says, this view is beautiful.

She puts her hands on the black metal of the balcony rail and leans over, looks down at the tiny patchwork squares of roof housing so many different people, so many different lives.

It would be such a long way to fall, she says.

Once she has started to say the word love, she cannot stop. They say it to each other countless times throughout the rest of the holiday, and even when they are silent, the word still chatters through her, out into her reaching fingers, her clutching lips.

It is over too soon, of course, as she knows it will be. Almost before she has a chance to realise it, they are already standing by the black snake of a baggage carousel, which is heaving and twisting into life with bags and the very end of this time together. They watch and wait.

I'm going to learn how to make that pasta thing, you know, she says, for when you next come over.

And just like that, she thinks of her little flat for the first time since leaving England, of the perfect, quiet coldness of it that had been so pleasing to her before, and is suddenly afraid.

Oh, she says, come *soon*.

His hand tightens on hers. I will, he says. As soon as I can. I promise.

Then he lets go and dives forward to collect her suitcase from the carousel belt, dropping it heavily at her feet.

They wheel their bags out together, past the deserted customs desk and the cluster of scrawled names on taxi signs, out on to the main concourse. This is where they must say goodbye. She has no idea how to do this. She quickens her pace and walks ahead slightly, towards the exit. If they must do it, let it be done soon.

Oh shit, she hears him say behind her, *shit*.

She drops the handle of her bag and turns around, but he is not there. There are so many people, so much movement. She turns around on the axis of her suitcase and scans the circling faces, but she cannot see the one she recognises. She is alone. For one indignant second, she considers walking on towards the exit, as she would have done if she had been by herself. And then she spots, just as if it was a clue in a children's puzzle book left there for her to find, a tuft of familiar grey-seeded hair behind a magazine rack in the open shop front next to her. She seeks it out.

He is standing very still behind the rack, fixing his gaze firmly on the open magazine he holds in front of him.

What are you doing? she says.

The furtive, frowning shape of his green eyes is unfamiliar to her. She does not know what to say to him.

It's Chris, this new, anxious him says, with urgent quietness.

Chris?

Anna's brother. Chris, he says. I should have thought – he often flies out from here to see clients.

He looks over the top of the rack, still clutching the magazine. It's all right now, I think. He looked like he was on his way out. Best stay here for a few more minutes though. Or, well, I should, at least.

You want me to go? she says.

He puts the magazine back in the rack, smoothing the cover with unnecessary care, before looking directly back at her.

You know that's the last thing I want, he says, but yes, maybe you should. There's no point the two of us skulking around. He starts to fumble in his pocket. Look, I was going to do this outside at the rank, but here, take a cab home, do.

She stops his hand, pressing it still in his jacket pocket. You don't need to do that, she says.

No, please, I'd like to. If I could, I'd be driving you.

Really, I'd prefer it, she says, if you didn't. I can get myself home.

Shit, he says again. He looks older, sadder, more tired. Look, I'll call you. As soon as I can.

All right, she says. She is suddenly, bitterly, tired too, with a grey weariness that seems to seep out of her, in her breath, in her hands, in every word she says. She starts to think about how she feels, and then realises she does not want to think, she wants to sleep. She lets herself think only of her bed, of the white, clean smell of sheets.

Hey – he says, and touches her arm as she moves to leave. I'm sorry to do that to you. So sorry. I'm not used to – all this. I just panicked. But he can't see us. You know he can't.

I know, she says.

Whenever she remembers that holiday afterwards, she thinks of sun on red tiles, and heavy blue quilts, and pale faraway hills, and looking at the peachy skin of painted women, with his voice close in her ear. And then always, last and most vividly, she recalls standing alone in that crowded hallway, new love thrumming uselessly in her bones.

*

1995

'A show?' Clare said. 'What sort of show?'

'Don't get too excited,' Harriet warned her. 'It's a lot less fun than it sounds. Dad makes us go every year.' She rolled back over the arm of the sofa, landing in the cushions with a soft *whump*.

'It's fun, you know it is,' Tom said. 'Or at least you seemed to be having fun, last year.'

'That was last year.' Harriet stared up at the ceiling, kicking her heels against the side of the sofa. 'This year is totally different.'

After the first few days, Harriet had suddenly become

friendly towards them both – or as friendly as Harriet could be, anyway. Whether this was because she had decided they were all right really, or whether this was a last, lonely act of teen desperation, Clare couldn't tell. Josie and Anna seemed pleased that they were all spending time together, but Clare wasn't so sure. Friendly Harriet made her more nervous than grumpy Harriet. And it meant that it had become even harder for her to find times to talk to Tom about everything, when Harriet wasn't going to overhear.

'There's lots of things to see,' Tom said, 'like animals, and cars, and they have a fairground, with a big slide. And a funhouse.'

'Yeah, the fairground is the only exciting thing,' Harriet conceded, 'but I bet Mum won't let us go in the funhouse this year.'

'She won't let you go again, anyway,' Tom said quietly. 'Not after last time.'

'Oh piss off,' Harriet muttered.

'Why, what happened in the funhouse?' Clare said, at the same time, before she thought not to ask it. She was always doing this to Josie too, she knew, but she couldn't seem to stop it happening. There was nothing she could do now – the words were out, and she watched them roll over and across Harriet's face, where they slapped her mouth into a scowl.

'Never mind,' Harriet said. 'It doesn't matter.'

Tom shrugged. 'Well, anyway, I bet me and Clare could go in, if we liked.'

There was a small, loud silence, in which Clare looked slowly from one to the other. 'It sounds fun,' she said carefully. And then, more carefully, 'I don't think I've ever been to a show like this before.'

'It's a proper country thing,' Harriet said. 'Every farmer

on the island goes, I bet. Lots of men in those stupid green jackets and wellies.'

An image of Jem flickered into Clare's head, and she shuddered. She couldn't help but look at Tom. He was staring back at her, and she knew he could see the same image, hanging there over both of them.

'I reckon it's the highlight of their year,' Harriet said in disgust, and turning over on the sofa, pressed her face into the back of the seat. 'It'll be completely boring, you'll see, unless—' The last words were lost, muffled by the cushions, and neither Clare nor Tom asked her to repeat them.

'They have others on the island,' Marcus said, 'but the West Show is the biggest, I think. And the most fun.'

'I warn you now, Marcus likes best to look at all the vegetables. Prize-winning marrows, and those ridiculous vegetable sculptures,' Anna said. 'You know, Queen Elizabeth made out of a courgette and some carrots, that sort of thing.'

They were walking from the place where they had parked the car, in an endless grass field, over towards the point of a white tent that served as the entrance. Anna had linked her arm through Marcus's, and was leaning into his shoulder, swinging a wide-brimmed straw hat with her other hand. She kept trying to put it on, but the breeze would whip at the edges until she took it off again, with a tiny, painted pout of frustration.

Josie walked beside Anna, and Clare stayed close beside her, just as Josie had told her to do. 'It'll be busy, bug. I don't want to lose you.'

All three of them – Clare, Tom and Harriet – had been briefed in the car by Anna about the Lost Children tent.

'I'm too old to be a Lost Child now,' Harriet said.

'Well I'm very sorry there's no Lost Teenager tent especially for you,' Anna said, with a high, acid note to her voice, 'but we'll just all have to make do. Just make sure you stick together, kids, okay?'

'Well, that's just bloody great,' Harriet said, to the glass of the window, but all the same, she was now walking obediently next to Tom, using the occasional step to kick at a tuft of grass.

'I'll have you know,' Marcus said, 'some of those vegetable sculptures are masterpieces.'

Josie gave her dry chuckle. 'I must admit, this is not something I thought I'd be seeing on this holiday,' she said, 'or well, ever, really.'

'See, Marcus?' Anna said. 'It's just you who likes them. Just you and your queens made out of carrots.'

This struck all of them as funny, even though Anna hadn't meant it to be. But it was a sunny, breezy day, and everyone was suddenly laughing.

Once they had paid for tickets and come through the white tent, they were standing in another large, grassy enclosure, flanked on each side by the white canvas of long tents and small tables furnished with cakes and bric-a-brac and signs. The garish fronts of the funfair were visible in the distance. There were people everywhere – and not just Harriet's farmers, either – couples hand in hand, families with pushchairs, clusters of children chattering and pushing from stand to stand. A puffed-up megaphone voice drifted over from a roped-off area, which had people crowded around it. Somewhere, a bright, three-note tune was playing over and over.

Tom and Harriet wandered a little apart, following the trail of people from table to table. Clare pressed closer to

Josie. 'All right, bug?' her mother said. 'It's big, isn't it? What do you want to do?'

'Shall we do Marcus's vegetables first?' Anna said. 'So we can get them over with?' There was a playful teasing to her voice.

Marcus grabbed her around her waist. 'Come on then, you. I'll make you look at every single one.'

Clare felt Josie's fingers suddenly tighten on her shoulder.

'Kids,' Anna called back to her children, 'come on this way, first.'

'Can't we split up?' Harriet said, coming back towards them. 'There's *dogs* over there. Jumping through things.'

'We've been through this. You're not going off on your own, Harriet.'

'Why don't I take them over, Anna?' Josie said. 'To see the dogs. You go off to the tents. We'll catch you up inside.'

'Oh you crafty thing, Jos.' Anna giggled. 'I wish I could come too. But there's no escape for me.' She did not look at all as if she meant this.

'Thanks, Josie,' Marcus said, still with his arm bound around Anna's waist.

'It's no trouble,' Josie said, pulling Clare still closer to her. 'It's no trouble at all.' As Marcus and Anna walked away, Clare wriggled free from her mother's grasp, and Josie sighed.

It turned out to be the dogs that everybody was watching in the central enclosure. The warbling megaphone voice belonged to a portly man wearing a red fleece, commenting on the dogs' progress as they raced round the square, jumping up and over a series of fences, balancing from one end of a seesaw to another, climbing up steps and sliding through tubes. Each owner ran the course beside their dog, calling and whistling to it as it dashed and skittered and occasionally wobbled through the obstacles.

The audience let Clare and the others slip in, near to the rope, Josie hovering a little behind.

'Oh,' said Harriet, 'look at the black one!'

'They're clever,' Tom said, 'aren't they?'

'They know exactly where to go,' Clare said. 'They must have practised a lot.'

'I wish we could have a dog.' Harriet ran the thread of the rope through her fingers. 'We could train it to do that. Couldn't we, Tom?'

Tom didn't answer. 'Tom?' Harriet said again. 'Tom? Couldn't we?'

She and Clare both turned to look at him at the same time. He was standing very still, with his dark-white look, staring past the rushing dog and owner into the crowd on the other side of the rope.

'God, you're so weird,' Harriet muttered, and returned her attention to the leaping dog.

'What is it?' Clare said to him, quietly, tentatively.

Tom did not move his head at all. 'I thought I saw him, for a second, right here.'

'Where?' Clare followed his look out across the line of faces along the rope. She scanned over the rows of eyes, noses, mouths, the concentration, the delight, the laughter. None of these expressions belonged to Jem.

'Tom, I don't see him.'

'He's here,' Tom said in a whisper. 'I know it. We have to keep away from him.'

'We will,' Clare replied, feeling a tight panic climb up into her chest. 'And we can make sure we stay with Mum and your parents, all day.'

'That won't help us.' Tom finally turned his head, and

lifted his eyes to hers. 'Don't you get it yet?' he asked, firmly, but not unkindly. 'With this, the grown-ups can't help us at all.'

Clare bit her lip. She tried to imagine explaining to Josie, and knew what Tom said was true. She bravely looked back, once more, across the ring. In front of them, a brown and white dog leapt high, daring, through a hoop.

After that, of course, Clare began to search through all the faces they passed. There were a lot of them, but she and Tom tried to look up and around at every one. Harriet complained they were slowing everyone down, and even the parents told them twice not to dawdle, but all the same, it was hard to stop looking, once they had started.

'He could be anywhere,' Tom said, as they left the dog show, and these words haunted Clare, stalking her in and out of each tent, up and down each display of vegetables and jam jars and painted landscapes, between stalls and ice creams and gaggles of people pointing and buying and clutching bags and candyfloss.

Marcus did show them the vegetable sculptures, in the end, ranged down a long aisle of trestle tables in the warm, plastic air of the end tent. 'See,' he said to Clare and Josie, 'tell me they're not brilliant.'

He made space for Clare, so she could walk down beside him along the front of the tables and look, and she did her best to concentrate, despite the line of faces creeping slowly down the aisle opposite. Short, stubby penguins with marrow bodies and carrots for beaks and feet and skis, a cauliflower dog and broccoli cat, Bob Marley, with his hair made entirely from corn and grated courgettes.

Anna rolled her eyes, but Josie laughed. '*Cob* Marley,' she said, reading the sign. 'All right, Marcus, you win.'

'Oh don't encourage him, Jos,' Anna said loudly, behind, but Marcus grinned back at her.

'I'm glad to have at least one other fan. How about you, Clare?'

'I like them,' she said, not really caring that much either way, but wanting to please him, because Josie had pleased him too. And after all, they were fun and colourful, and it was a relief to look at a row of silly faces with grape eyes and clownish carrot mouths that did not have danger hiding within them. She could almost forget, for a moment, that Jem existed.

'That's my girl,' Marcus said.

The funfair was saved until the end of the day, perhaps because it was in the furthest part of the field, or perhaps because there was a sense that Anna did somehow not quite approve of it. Clare was not sure why she was so scathing about the rides and the people who used them, but once they had reached the area, Marcus and Josie seemed happy enough to come in with them and dole out a couple of pounds apiece for the merry-go-rounds and helter-skelters, and rickety little train cars that ran up and around and down a twisting, yellow track. They left Anna standing by a snack kiosk, in charge of three red helium balloons that had been handed out to Clare, Tom and Harriet free by a local insurance company.

'Don't be too long,' Anna said. 'And don't let them go on any of the big rides, Marcus. You know the ones.'

She looked mistrustfully up at a spinning, screeching wheel of spokes and legs and arms, which tilted back and forth above the gaudy roof of the carousel.

'Don't worry, my darling,' Marcus said. 'We'll look after them. Are you sure you won't come with us?'

'You know I hate these places,' Anna said. 'You *know*.'

Marcus leant forwards and kissed her, quickly, intently. 'We won't be long, I promise.' The balloons bobbed together over them.

And then they were free. First they all went on the big, old-fashioned merry-go-round, climbing up on the varnished horses, clutching at the twisted gilt poles, and feeling themselves rise and fall and turn, round and round. Josie took Clare on the striped green helter-skelter, sitting together on a rough horsehair mat that scratched the backs of Clare's legs. She clung to Josie's knees while her mother screamed above her, and they flew round and down to land in a laughing, shocked heap at the bottom. Harriet and Marcus disappeared to ride a giant, twisting, caged swing that flung them far up into the air and upside down, Harriet's hair a flash of buffeting red behind the bars.

'And we'll go on the bumper cars, of course,' Marcus said, when he rejoined the others, Harriet breathless and tousled and jubilant beside him, and he took them all swerving off around the little ring, driving the bright bubbles of cars, in a battery of bumps and sparks.

'That was my favourite,' Tom said, hopping from foot to foot, 'my absolute favourite thing.'

Clare grinned at him. The rides and screams seemed to have knocked all the dark anxiety out of him. It was so easy to believe that Jem could not be here, among all the colours and melodies and flashing lights. And despite their careful searching, they had not seen a single person who could have been him all day.

'Do you want to go again?' Marcus said, looking down at his flushed, pleased son.

'We've done that one,' Tom said. 'I want to do the fun-house now.'

'Me too,' Harriet said, coming around the other side of her father.

Marcus turned between them, a small frown deepening between his eyebrows. 'Are you sure that's a good idea, Harri?' he said.

Harriet put her hands on her hips, her elbows sticking out. 'God, you sound just like Mum,' she said. 'Come on, Dad, that was a whole *year* ago.' The words were hers, but the elbows, the hips, the indignation, were Anna's.

'All the same,' Marcus said, 'I – and I'm sure your mum too – would rather you didn't.'

'I want to go,' Tom said suddenly, 'I really want to go. *Really.*'

'If he can go, I can go,' Harriet said. 'Otherwise it's not fair. You know it's not.'

Marcus looked up at Josie, standing next to Clare. 'What about you two?' he said. 'What do you think, Josie?'

Josie shrugged. 'I really don't mind either way, Marcus,' she said. 'Do you want to go, Clare?'

Clare glanced at Tom, into his keen gaze. 'If Tom goes, I think I'd like to go too.'

'See?' Harriet said.

Marcus gave a big, exaggerated sigh that moved through his entire body. 'Fine,' he said, 'fine. I give in. Harriet, you and Tom can go, but on one condition – I go in with you too.'

Harriet and Tom turned to each other and grinned. It was the first time Clare had seen them do that. She realised, suddenly, how much time you must spend with a brother or sister, all those days, mealtimes, weeks, holidays, years in the same rooms as each other, with the same conversations and games and books. It was something she could not ever imagine doing.

'And we stick together,' Marcus said. 'Is that clear?'

He did not get an answer. Harriet and Tom had already set off for the funhouse queue, side by side. Clare followed them, running, just a little, to catch up.

Marcus paid for them all, at the ticket booth. 'Really,' Josie kept saying, 'really.'

'No, no, this one is entirely the fault of my horrible children,' Marcus kept replying. 'This one is definitely on me.'

'You all together?' said the man standing at the entryway, which was a giant clown face with a bulging nose and a grinning, gaping mouth, and together, Marcus and Josie answered 'Yes'.

The children all ran ahead, but Marcus stepped back, to let Josie go first through the lurid, painted lips.

The funhouse was a maze of ramps tilted at odd angles, and walkways that slid out from under your feet as you came down them, and lurid punchbags that swung back and heavily into you as you fought your way past. Clare and Tom and Harriet lost the parents here, leaving them behind somewhere among the swinging colours, and by the time they had climbed the ladder to the spiral slide, and come laughing, shooting down again, breathless, into another part of the funhouse entirely, Josie and Marcus were nowhere to be seen.

'Should we wait?' Clare said, but the others only shrugged.

'They'll catch up,' Harriet said. 'Come on.'

They followed a chattering line of T-shirts and trainers through the inside of a turning tube. Harriet made a great show of squealing and swaying, but Clare took satisfaction in realising how to walk into the turn of the floor, how to keep herself still and proudly upright.

'It's the mirrors next!' Tom said, as he stumbled out after her.

'Yes, all right,' said Harriet, a little terse. 'We all know it's the mirrors.' She stalked off into the next room. Tom grabbed Clare's arm with one chilly hand.

'That was it, you see,' he said, quietly, quickly. 'It was the mirrors. Harriet freaked out.'

'Why?' Clare said.

'She thought she saw me – you know – disappear.'

'And did she?'

Tom nodded. 'They said she must have been imagining it, that the mirrors can play tricks on you. But there's sometimes ways in through them too. If you get it right.'

A dark tingle began at Clare's fingers, and crept up and through her body. 'Will you show me?' she asked.

'I'll try,' Tom said. 'I'm really not sure how it works. But I'll try.'

He stayed close to her as they stepped through the doorway and into the hall. Clare blinked and saw the two of them reflected back towards her in a thousand tiny, silver-dark pieces.

There was nothing here except them and their bodies, bouncing off each other and into each other, down long corridors of Clares and Toms who moved and spun with an uncanny synchronicity. The floor was black, and the ceiling was black, with spots of cold, white light, and all around them the figures turned and looked and smiled. Occasionally other people moved into the frames, their reflections dancing against her own, but she could not tell where they were. She spotted Harriet whisking in and out a few times, a flash of red hair in the dark.

Clare saw the back of her own head, the neat smooth-
ness of the bob of her hair, and marvelled. And watched
herself marvel, there, at the same time, in the glass. This,
in itself, was magic, even thought it was all quite real, quite
ordinary, when you really thought about it.

'How do we get through?' she said.

'Let's keep going,' Tom said, and when she halted,
puzzled by the circle of corridors, he took her hand and
started to walk, with an authority that impressed her.

There was a feeling here, but it was all jumbled up with
the darkness and the mirrors and the amazement. She let
Tom lead her on and through, looking around and into her
own eyes, wide and black. They blinked, wondering, back
at her, from a hundred different faces.

'Oh!' Tom said, abruptly, and let go of her hand.

His reflections rippled out of sight beside her and
vanished.

For a second, she did not speak, just in case he came
back. 'Tom?' she said, and reached out for his arm, but met
only glass. She started to stretch out, pressing her hands
against every surface she met, but every one of them was
cold and glossy and hard. Her hand scrabbled against desperate hand after desperate hand, but there was nothing
else there apart from her own searching figure.

He'll come back, she thought, he knows how. For a
second, she thought of Harriet standing here last year,
Harriet who *didn't* know, and felt sympathy for her. She
looked up at her own face in the glass and pressed both
sets of fingertips to those of her reflection, steepling them
together. She smiled at herself, and she smiled back.

'Well, I suppose I should wait here for him,' she said to
herself, out loud, which was fine. But then Clare in the
mirror tilted her head slightly to one side, and gave an extra

half of a smile, which Clare in the real world was sure she was not giving in return.

She drew back sharply from the glass. Mirror Clare fell back too, but did she do it in exactly the same way, at exactly the same time? She dared to move a little left, a little right, and Mirror Clare did the same, but was it with a twist of the hips that was entirely her own? 'Tom?' she said again. 'Tom?' Her voice was trembling, and came out higher than she was expecting.

A cluster of people jostled past her, giggling and jumping. Their limbs filled the world around her with noisy movement. Mirror Clare stopped still and stared back at her, impassive.

'Where is he?' she said, when the crowd had passed, to herself who was not really herself at all. 'Why won't you show me?'

Mirror Clare was silent, mocking. A shiver bent itself around her spine.

'Why hello there, little miss,' came a deep voice behind her. 'Have you lost all your friends, now?'

A thousand dark Jems loomed into being around her. In the mirror, every Clare opened her mouth and screamed. She staggered back, both away and towards the figures, and then collided with a solid body, all movement and roundness and a pair of arms that fell round her shoulders to enfold her.

'Hey, bug, what in the world is it?' Josie said. 'Hey, it's all right. It's all right.' Clare clung to her one mother, to the single curve of her waist, to her every real, present breath.

7

A Secret Revealed

Easter comes late this year, on a warm weekend almost tipping into summer, daffodils already shrivelling into mustard skins on their stalks.

He will not see her over the holiday. It is family time, of course. Everyone knows this, from her office mates discussing plans over a scaled-shut, hissing kettle in the kitchen to the supermarket advertisements with their mothers, fathers and broods of cheerful, squabbling children. She pictures him sitting opposite Anna at a dining room table, Harriet and her partner smiling between them, a smooth linen cloth, a plate of pink lamb, two neat salt and pepper shakers. It is to be expected.

So she goes home too, as she must, as is expected.

Only it is not expected by Josie. Her mother has long since given up on expectations, of any kind. She now lives in a small, square semi, with a mortgage and two narrow bedrooms and a living room that is full of sunlight and hard, useful furniture. They moved so often from flat to flat when she was young that her mother became very good at discarding any object without a purpose, and even though now Josie has a house that is unassailably her own, she still keeps her shelves and cupboards as free as possible.

It's not a palace, but it'll do for me, Josie always says. A roof over my head that's all mine.

Just because it's not a palace doesn't mean you can't hang a few pictures, she always retorts. And gradually, over the past few years, some bright artist prints have climbed on to the walls, a few flowered china dishes from Spain sidled on to the mantelpiece, a cheerful patterned rug crept into the hallway to cover the rough boards.

It's clutter, Josie says, just clutter, but all the same, she sometimes notices her mother looking up for a moment at the sunflower painting above the fireplace, when the afternoon light catches on the yellow, and so she continues to talk about bedspreads and tablecloths and silk flowers for the grate.

She rings her mother one grey Saturday morning after Marcus has just left. I was thinking about coming to visit for Easter, she says. If you're around, that is.

Oh, I'm always around, you know that.

Well, you know, you might have plans, she says, a little shortly. I wouldn't want to disrupt anything.

Fifty miles away, Josie gives her sharp, dry laugh. You won't be disrupting me at all, you know that. Come home, bug, her mother says, come home.

She closes her eyes against the sudden, surprising tears this brings. They tingle under her eyelids.

Josie picks her up from the station, just as she has always done, in the car that smells of mints and must and trips to Yorkshire. Before she gets off the train, she turns her phone to silent. He has not texted today, but there is always the possibility he will. She knows if she hears the message arrive, she will not be able to resist the desire to read, to reply, to treasure it, even with her mother sitting there next to her.

As she gets into the car, her mother leans over to touch her lips briefly against her cheek, before starting the car again and pulling out into the road.

So how've you been, then? Josie says. You look tired. Busy at work?

Fairly, she says. It's a bit of a rush to get everything out in time for the new syllabus. But we'll get there.

Oh right, Josie says. Oh yes. I'm sure you will.

She knows her mother doesn't really understand what this means, but she does not ask her to explain further, and for once, this is pleasing. The thought required to form every word suddenly seems too much of an effort. She rests her head back against the seat.

And you? she says to Josie. How is everything here?

Her mother gives the little, dry laugh again. Oh, you know, the same as ever. The same as ever.

And everything is the same as ever, at least on the outside. The little house sits as solidly as it ever did, in the warm, quiet hum of a cul-de-sac on a Friday afternoon. She takes out her suitcase from the boot of the car, while Josie goes through the familiar motions of the key in the lock, the flip of the alarm cupboard, the chink of the key in the dish on the bookcase.

Tea, then? Josie says, as she does after every arrival, and picks up the kettle.

Oh, yes please, she says. The tap still spits water unevenly to one side, and as always, as she has to, she feels moved to add, I can't believe you still haven't got that fixed.

The movements, the words, the offering, are all parts of a ritual that has been theirs for years, since the day she left for university. This is how they show their affection for each other. She has played her part now, and all that is left is to rest her elbows on the table and drink the tea her mother brings to her, in a mug selected because it has no chip in the rim. Despite everything that has happened back there to her life in her little flat, this place here will always, irrevocably, continue to be the same. She sips her tea.

So then, Josie says. What do you want to do this weekend?

I hadn't really thought, she says.

Her mother blows across the top of her mug to cool it, pursing her lips. Well, she says, I need to do some things in the garden. You could help me, if you like.

All right, she says.

You don't have to. We can go do something else. And you know there's still that whole heap of your books upstairs too, if you'd rather sit and read.

No, it would be nice to be outside, she says. I don't get a chance to be out much, in the city.

You always did like to get out, Josie says. I still can see you now, tramping around Nan's garden with those cats.

So let's do the garden, then, she says. It's a lovely day.

Josie sits back. All right. And we'll need to go to the supermarket too, later, to get something for our tea. I don't know what you like these days.

I like the same things I always did, she says.

Even as she says it, she realises this is not quite the truth.

Later, after she has tackled the strip of garden, scrubbing around for the nubs of weed in the dirt, and steered a trolley through the chill of the supermarket aisles, adjudicating on her mother's decisions about meals, she and Josie say goodnight, and she is finally alone, in the bedroom which is considered to be hers.

The heating has gone off some time ago, and the room is cold. It is a thin room, painted in a plain grey cream,

with a tall wardrobe fixed into one narrow end and a
bed wedged in the centre, guarding the wardrobe door.
It smells of dust and cardboard, and has the stillness of a
place where there has been no life for many months. She
wraps herself in the duvet on the bed and searches for her
phone in her bag.

There is a text waiting for her in the silence, as she
thought there might be. It crept in this afternoon, as she
was pressing her fingers purposefully into the soil. He loves
her, he misses her, he wishes he was there with her. He does
not, she notes wryly, wish she was there with him.

She sends a text back, saying all the right things. I love
you, I miss you, I wish you were here too. And she does,
although she dreads the machinations that would have to
happen to bring him here.

It is 10 p.m. He is probably already in his own bed, next
to Anna, lying above a houseful of food and people and
plans for his weekend. She puts the phone back in her bag
and refuses to wait for a reply.

Instead, she gets back out of the bed and kneels to look
under it. The boxes are still there, in the same arrangement as they were when she'd slid them in, years ago, with
writing in black marker pen on their sides. MUM, DON'T
YOU DARE THROW THESE AWAY!

She pulls them out, one after the other, the cardboard
bottoms of the boxes catching on the rough carpet. Here
are her childhood books, packed away one summer in a fit
of teenage scorn and not brought out since. She lifts the
flaps of the boxes and brings stacks of them out, piling
them up on the floor around her. They are all still here,
all these books she treasured, all the stories of magic and
quests and witches and beautiful plots with certain, rea-
soned endings. All these other worlds that existed so close

to her own, that were almost within reach. They have only been sleeping here, waiting for her to return.

When she tells him her stories now, she wonders if her memories have been coloured in by these books, so skilfully that even she cannot distinguish the lines beneath them. She was so vividly sure, at the time, of what they were doing, but now she doubts herself every time she thinks of it. And of course, Tom is not there to corroborate her story.

There is a precedent here, in these musty pages, for everything – the mirrors, the caves, the darkness in the corner of the cupboards. She sits in the circle of stories she has created and pulls her knees close to her chest.

She cannot go back. All she has, really, is these half-memories, with threads of doubt strung through them, and the stray, uncertain patches of darkness, which still flicker occasionally in the corner of rooms. That is all she will ever have, now.

It is hard to keep believing in something you have no real proof ever existed. It is perhaps easier if you can not. If you can focus on the real things that are happening in this life, not another one. She starts to stack the books back into the boxes, carefully, respectfully, decidedly.

I need to tell you something, she says.

She is with Josie the next morning, after breakfast. They have finished the washing-up and are sitting opposite each other, the Saturday newspaper dismantled between them.

Josie looks up from the magazine supplement, and gives her a small, sharp stare. What is it? Are you sick?

I'm not sick, she says.

Well, then, what is it?

She takes a deep, shaking, breath. This will not be easy, however long she leaves it. I'm seeing someone, she says.

Oh, Josie says, well, that's good? Isn't it? Her mother's voice is deliberately softened, casual.

She straightens the pages of the paper in front of her before replying. Sort of, she says. It's not ideal.

Oh god, bug, Josie says then, in her normal tone, just come out with it. And if you're trying to tell me you're a lesbian, you *know* I don't care about that.

No, no, I'm not, she says. It's a him. It's just that, well, you know him. Knew him.

So who is he?

It's Marcus, she says quietly, and then louder, Marcus Chilcott.

She cannot look at her mother's face, so she looks down instead, at her fingers criss-crossing over the lines of newsprint.

Josie laughs, higher than usual. No. This is a joke, isn't it? Come on. Marcus? No. He's – no – and he's older than me.

It's not a joke, she says. You know how we bumped into each other, in the city, that one time. Well, it just sort of happened.

She dares to look up. Josie is very still, her mouth pulled into a tiny, whitening line.

It wasn't meant to, she says. Neither of us meant it to happen at all.

But it did, Josie says.

Please, she says, I don't want to upset you.

Josie pushes back her chair, scraping along the tiles. You don't want to upset *me*! Christ. I suppose he's still married to Anna too?

He says they're not really together, she begins, that they're really leading separate lives—

Oh, come on now, for fuck's sake, Josie says. Don't be

an idiot. That's what they *all* say. Grow up, Clare. And Marcus, of all people? Jesus.

Please, she says again.

Her mother stands up. I can't do this. Not now. I'm going out.

Josie walks out. The keys screech against the china of the dish, the front door slams, and the car is kicked into life.

She sits and listens to the car engine until it fades out of the street, and then folds her arms on the newspaper and rests her head down over them. She breathes into the ink and paper of the words. It is done.

She cannot sit and wait for her mother to return, listening to every car in the distance, so she picks up the key under the plant pot, which has lived there ever since she was a teenager (second from right, round the back by the tree, for use only in *emergencies*, do you hear?) and ventures out. The click of the front door echoes round the cul-de-sac, and then there is silence again. She starts to walk, and the sound of her steps follows her down the tarmac, and out, left, on to a longer road flanked with square, evenly pitched bungalows, painted in pinks and greys and creams. None of these houses looks quite real, with their neat doorways, and cars parked sedately in each driveway. There are people living here, there must be people living here, but where are they all? She imagines them hiding below the sill of each long frame, peering out at her through the glass, being careful not to tremble the blinds. The walker, the stranger, the outsider. She lifts her head higher, walks more boldly, dares to slow and stare at each blank window she passes.

Such a lovely day. They are probably all out, with their families. She knows that.

She walks until she has managed to lose herself, in a maze of houses that all look the same, and then she turns, and retraces her steps until she arrives back at the right house, in the right cul-de-sac.

As she walks up to the front door, she hears a car coming down the road, round and into the drive behind her, scraping to a stop in front of the steps. She puts the key in the lock, and does not turn round. A car door opens and shuts.

I took the key, she says, under the pot.

Is that still there? Josie says. Christ. I'd forgotten. I should probably move that.

It might come in handy, she says. You never know. She holds the door open for her mother, without looking up at her.

Josie comes in after her, and shuts the door firmly. Look, Clare, she says, I was shocked. But I had every right to be shocked, you must admit that.

I'm not expecting you ever to like it, she says, still looking down and away.

Like it! You're bloody right I won't ever like it.

But it's happened, she goes on, a little more steadily. So I had to tell you.

But now what, Clare? Now what? Josie seizes her chin, and makes her look up and into her sharp, narrowed eyes. Is this just going to continue like this forever, now? Are you going to carry on seeing each other every so often, when he's 'on business'? Sneak away, at the last minute, for the odd Saturday night? Spend every weekend thinking about what he might be doing, at home with his family, in the garden on a Sunday afternoon?

It is all uncomfortably familiar. She pulls her chin back out of her mother's grasp.

But it's not like that, she says, with us. It's different. He's different.

He's the same as any other bloody man, Josie says. And now I'll tell you now what. Now you'll get pregnant, and it will all be one unholy mess. There are bright tears in her eyes.

She has to move away, then, from Josie. *I* was an unholy mess, then? she says.

Shit, Josie says. Oh, shit. No, not you. Never you.

But that's what happened, isn't it? she says. He was married. That's why you'll never talk about it.

Josie dips her head. The frame of her shoulders seems smaller than ever. Yes, she says, he was married. He was older, and he was married. He had – has children. Older children. And when it happened, he didn't want another one. He …

She wishes for a Place. One, right here, in the corner of the step, that she could crawl right into and never come out from.

Josie kneels down beside her. Clare, she says, he never knew you. He never even met you. If he had—

Her mother breaks off, and reaches out to her. Look, I was angry too. He didn't want me. He didn't want us. So I took us away, out of it. Maybe he would have come round, in time. But I couldn't risk it.

Josie takes her hands in her own, and presses her fingertips, one by one.

I'll never be sorry I had you, not for a second. But I don't want the same for you. I took us away because I never wanted you ever to be *not wanted*, by anyone.

They do not talk about it again that weekend. They are good at not talking. They make tea, they read the paper, they cook the meat they have chosen together. Josie puts her back on the train on Sunday evening.

It is getting dark as they stand together on the platform, waiting for the bright orange minutes to count themselves down on the screen above them.

You don't have to stay, she says.

I'll stay, Josie says. I want to.

A minute flicks from one to the next.

At least it's been nice, she says. Nice weather. It's good to see the sun.

Clare, Josie says suddenly, a little sharp, we could try and find him, you know. Get in touch. I wouldn't mind. If you want.

No, she says. I don't think so. And then, as an after-thought, thank you.

Well, all right, Josie says. But the offer's there. If you change your mind.

It is exactly as if she has just refused a drink or another biscuit. She smiles at the absurdity of it.

I never do know what you're smiling at, Josie says. You'd think I'd have learnt, after all this time.

The track whistles beneath them as the train comes nearer, two bright points of light in the gloom. Josie pulls her suddenly close, pressing her lips to her cheek. My bug, she says, my bug.

And this is as near as Josie will get to saying I love you. She takes the kiss, the pet name, the cups of tea.

On the train, speeding away from Josie, she lets herself think again about the man who did not want her. Who did not want, in the end, either of them. Hasn't she always known this must have been the case? The fact he was not there was proof enough. It changes nothing, to know this for sure.

But Marcus is not this man. Marcus is another man. A different man. She knows this. She presses her forehead to the dark window, and closes her eyes against the reflections in the glass.

*

1995

'I'll stay, if you want me to,' Josie said. 'I don't have to go out.'

'I told you,' Clare said, 'I'm fine.' She knew Josie did want to go out, really.

'Well, we've given Alexa the number of the restaurant, you know. And you know how to use the phone in the hall, don't you? If there's anything ...'

'I know,' Clare said.

Josie had been hovering over her ever since she had carried her out of the mirrors and into the light, pressing Clare closer than normal and, over the top of her head, apologising profusely to everyone else, Marcus, Jem, the man from the funhouse kiosk.

'It happens all the time,' the man kept saying, a little defensively. 'Kids get spooked. There is a warning up.'

'Even Harriet got a scare last year, didn't you?' Marcus said. Harriet, behind him, shrugged.

Jem just gave his odd little chuckle. Clare looked down at the ground, her mother's hand shielding her cheek.

'But you're all right now, aren't you, Clare?'

'There's a *warning* up,' the man from the kiosk said again, raising his hands and turning away from them all, and back to the line of people.

The grown-ups were going out for dinner, without them. 'Escaping,' Anna called it. She had arranged it all. A girl called Alexa was coming to babysit – she was the daughter of the landlady, and according to Anna, she seemed 'lovely, responsible, a charming girl'.

'Oh, there's no need for that. I can stay, honestly,' Josie said. 'You and Marcus go on and have a lovely time together. And maybe I should, anyway, if Clare's not feeling well.'

'Nonsense, Jos,' Anna said. 'You come out with us. Treat yourself to a night off. Clare's all right, aren't you?'

'I'm fine,' Clare said again. It was all she could say.

'You didn't have to make such a fuss,' Tom said, just before teatime. 'You were just like Harri.'

She was shocked at the disgust in his voice. How could he be annoyed with *her*? 'You vanished!' she said. 'You just vanished and I couldn't get through. And then Jem turned up. It was like he *knew*. But you left me there.'

'I came back,' Tom said, aggrieved. 'I couldn't help going through.' Even now, he was a little light, a little joyous, with the same excitement he had shown on that first day in the cave. He had found one and made it through, and that was all that seemed to matter to him.

'But why couldn't you take me with you?' Clare asked. 'Like you said you would?'

Tom sat back on his heels for a moment. 'I don't know. It's interesting, isn't it?'

'It was really scary,' Clare said vehemently. 'That's what it was. I don't know what he might have done if Mum hadn't turned up in time.'

'You're annoyed, aren't you?' Tom said. 'I'm sorry I left you, but it wasn't my fault.'

'Anything could have happened,' Clare said.

'Okay, okay,' Tom said. 'It'll be different, I promise, next time.'

Then Anna and Josie swooped down on them, with scented, braceletted arms, to tell them goodnight, be good for Alexa, and remember to take out the pizzas in the oven.

Alexa was seventeen. She was wearing a strappy shift dress over a tight, white net top, a beaded choker around her neck. Her hair curved in a long, choppy bob and her fingernails were bright and painted. Harriet, who had been sulking about the need for a babysitter at all – 'can't you just give me the money to do it?' – suddenly sat up again on the sofa, animated, smoothing her fringe carefully.

Alexa perched on the edge of the coffee table and asked them all what year they were in school, what they'd been up to that day, if there was anything on television they wanted to watch tonight. Harriet butted in eagerly before Clare, every time, and Tom just shrugged.

'Mum put pizzas in,' Harriet said. 'For tea. Alexa, shall we go and sort it out?' Clare and Tom were clearly not invited.

'Good plan,' Alexa said. Harriet beamed and stood up, with what she considered to be her most sophisticated air, head held a little too high, and the two of them left the room.

'Where did you go to, then, this time?' Clare said, when the kitchen door had closed.

Tom pulled his knees to his chest and considered. 'It was the same place, I think, as before. All those lights, all that darkness. And the sounds. The same as the cave. Only—'

'Only?'

'It felt longer. Deeper. I could have gone on,' he said. 'Further in. If I'd wanted to.'

'And why didn't you?'

'It's like crawling into a crack,' he said. 'I thought I might get stuck. It's not always easy to turn round and get out again.'

'I would try and come and get you, you know,' Clare said, slightly shyly, 'if that happened.'

'Thanks,' Tom said.

They smiled at each other briefly, embarrassed, and then Harriet stalked in, hand on hip.

'Okay. So. The pizza is slightly burnt but you'll just have to eat round the burnt bits on the edges. Alexa says it's fine, she does that *all the time.*'

They ended up watching a film that happened to be on television about little flying robots from space, Harriet and Alexa tucked up at either end of the sofa, Clare in the armchair, and Tom cross-legged on the floor.

'There's room up here, buddy,' Alexa said, but Tom shook his head.

'He prefers the floor,' Harriet said, 'but that's because he's weird.'

'I'm sure that's not true,' Alexa exclaimed.

'Just ask anyone at school,' Harriet said.

Alexa pretended not to hear her. 'So have any of you guys seen this already? I don't think I have.'

'I have,' Harriet said. 'Loads of times. I love going to the cinema. I, like, do it all the time. Don't you?'

Alexa laughed. 'We don't have much choice here at the cinema. You're so lucky, living on the mainland. There's not a lot to do, really, out here.'

Clare tried to imagine living on the island all year round, after the tourists had gone. 'It must be really quiet,' she said out loud. 'Really, really quiet.'

'You can say that again,' Alexa said.

'I think I'd like it,' Clare said. She looked back at the robots whistling and zooming their way around a lady's kitchen, but in her head she saw herself standing on a tiny dot of crystal green, surrounded by sea and little, flickering patches of darkness.

The robots were taking over the apartment block, bit by bit. The people had been scared at first, but they were friendly robots, so it was all right, really. They were just finding this out when there came a knock at the door. They all looked round.

'I'll go,' Alexa said. 'You guys watch the film.'

She padded out. Her socks were thick and had little Snoopys all over them.

From the hall, Clare heard the door click open. She shivered, without knowing why.

'Oh hi!' she heard. 'How are you? – No, yeah, they're out. I'm sitting. – Yeah, a bit of extra cash! Did you want Mrs Chilcott? – Oh, yeah – no, I didn't know. At the West Show – Oh, poor kid. Yes, she seems fine. That's so sweet of you to pop over. I'd ask you in, but – Yeah – Yes, she's fine. – I'll tell them you came by. I will. Thanks. See you, Jem.'

Tom's head whipped round, and Clare started as Alexa closed the door again. She came treading softly back into the room.

'Who was that?' Harriet said.

'Oh, just Jem from round the corner,' Alexa said. 'You've met Jem, right? I think he wanted to see your parents. I'm sure he'll come back tomorrow, if it's important.'

'Oh, that crab guy,' Harriet said. 'He's a bit weird, isn't he?'

'Yeah, he can be a bit intense, but Jem's harmless,' Alexa said. 'I've known him all my life. He's always round here, with his fishing stuff.'

'He was at the Show today too,' Harriet said. 'I totally think he's stalking us.'

Alexa laughed again. 'No, that's island life for you. Honestly. Everyone's stalking everyone, round here.'

She and Harriet turned back to the television, but Clare could not help but watch the darkness in the corners of the room, crawling further inwards.

Alexa allowed them to stay up to see the end of the film, and then she sent them all to bed at the same time. Clare and Tom went, even as Harriet was still bargaining with Alexa for an extra half hour on the sofa.

'He's definitely following us,' Tom said to her, in the hallway. 'Here, the funfair, the beach, I know it.'

'But why?' Clare said. 'What does he want?'

Tom shook his head. 'I don't know. But it's got something to do with the Places. It must have. He's got that … that … feeling about him. You know what I mean.'

Clare nodded. 'Yes, but it's a bad one.' The shiver of seeing Jem was very similar to the feeling of realising a Place was nearby. Except that it made her feel scared and a little sick instead of pleasantly fearful. 'Like going to the dentist instead of going on a waterslide.'

'That's it,' Tom agreed. 'That's it exactly.'

'But what can we do?' Clare said. 'If he is following us, I mean.'

Tom frowned. 'Stay away from him, I suppose. That's all we can do. And I reckon we shouldn't let him see us go into any Places. That is, if Mum and Dad actually ever let us go and find any more.'

'I don't like it,' Clare said.

'Well, we can't do anything more about it tonight,' Tom said. 'So I suppose we may as well go to bed.'

For a second, Clare was jealous of Tom, who had the reassurance of sharing his bedroom with someone else, even if that someone was Harriet, while she had to climb the stairs and lie in that room alone, closing her eyes against anyone or anything that might come creeping up on her.

'Just yell,' Tom said, as if he was reading her thoughts. 'Just yell, and I'll come up. Our room's right under yours.'

Even so, it took her a few minutes to get up the confidence to climb the stairs, and enter the room. She made herself check the wardrobe, and under both beds, and once she'd satisfied herself there was nothing there except a few pale shadows, she undressed and dived into her bed, burying herself deep in the reassuring heaviness of the duvet. Her heart beat against the rustle of the material. She might never sleep, she thought.

She must have slept, in the end, because suddenly it was darker, and cooler, and car doors were slamming outside, footsteps scraping on the step. She rolled over and out of her cocoon of bedding, and lay alert, waiting for the next thing to happen.

'If you could just hang on here a few minutes, please,' Marcus's voice said, small and far below the windowsill, 'I'll just go and get our babysitter.'

She heard the front door slide open, chatter in the hallway.

'Alexa, I do hope you've got a brolly.' Josie's voice. 'It's raining cats and dogs out there now.'

'The taxi will take you on home,' Marcus, now. 'It's all right, I've paid him.'

'Honestly, Mr Chilcott—'

'No arguments. I want to make sure you get home safe.'

More chatter, and then the taxi started up, and drove away.

The voices hushed in the hallway now, reduced to mutters. 'She's in the garden. No, you just go to bed, Josie. I'll go out to her. It's all right. She does this a lot. I'll sort it out. Don't worry.'

As the footsteps came up the stairs, Clare rearranged herself into a plausible sleeping position, turned over on her side towards the window, eyes closed but both ears awake and listening. She was ready by the time her mother came into the room, tiptoeing into the new silence, placing her bag down on the dresser by the door.

She heard Josie sit down on the opposite bed, and then a series of small clinks and jingles that meant she was removing her bracelets and earrings, piece by piece. There was a sigh, and then her mother was still. In the quiet, the voices down below could be heard again – Marcus, deep and low, and Anna, shrill and fast and cutting over the top of him. If Clare listened hard, she could make out every word.

'I feel like – like – a third wheel, Marcus. All today. All every day. And with my own family.'

'Anna, come on. It's pissing it down. Anna.'

'You were laughing at me, Marcus. At *me*. It shouldn't be like that. And at the fair. Left holding those stupid bloody balloons for all that time. On my own.'

The bed creaked as Josie stood up again, and crossed over towards the window. The curtain rings clicked together. Clare risked opening her eyes. Her mother was leaning against the wall beside the window, twisting her head to look out. She had carefully hidden her face between the wall and the edge of the curtain, so she could not possibly be seen from outside.

'It's not how it's supposed to be, Marcus. I mean, Jesus.'

'Look, it was you who suggested this whole holiday thing. We could have come alone.'

'For fuck's sake, it's not about the holiday!' These words were louder, slicing right through the glass of the window-pane, and Josie flinched on the other side of it. 'It's *every* day. Having Josie here just makes it more clear.'

'Makes what more clear, exactly?'

'That you would rather be with anyone, anyone *at all*, who isn't me.'

'That's not true. Anna. Darling. You know that isn't true. Look, it's late, it's wet, we're tired. Let's discuss this in the morning, tomorrow, when we've all had—'

'It's always tomorrow. Always. Why can't you ever just talk about it right now?' Anna's voice had become a wail. She sounded exactly like Harriet. Clare did not even have to try to catch the words.

'Anna! Do you want the whole street to hear? Look, my stupid, darling Annie—' And Marcus's voice suddenly cut off into murmurs, and stillness, and murmurs again.

The figure at the window turned her head quickly away from the street, and pressed her back against the wall, arms crossed, a pillar of solid darkness on the night grey of the paint. She breathed loudly into the silence, pushing each breath out as if she wanted to be rid of it. She stood there for a very long time.

8

The Storm Comes

The next day, returning from the corner shop, she comes upon her neighbour Lilian with a cloud of candy-striped sheets, coming in from her side yard.

Caught them just in time, Lilian says. Did you ever see such a sky?

I know, she says in reply. It looks like it'll be a proper storm.

And it would be a bank holiday, of course, Lilian says. Isn't it always?

She is holding a pint of milk, one finger hooked through the cold, white ring of the handle. Her knuckle is pleasingly numb against it. Thunder, she says. I do like thunder.

Lillian laughs. Well, at least somebody's happy. She pushes her front door open and disappears into the long corridor, trailing pink and purple stripes.

As Lilian closes the door, there comes the first bright flash.

She makes a cup of tea, and watches the storm from her front window. The sky has darkened completely now, in a wave of bruises rolling over the rooftops. Lightning flashes on the slates, and then thunder rumbles over and under and through her. She counts between the flash and clap, just like she was taught to – one, two, three – a second for every mile away from the heart of the storm. She still doesn't know how true that is, although it would be easy to find out now, she supposes.

One, two. The hail starts to fall, clattering on to the roof and the tops of cars below, and pooling in tiny, crystalline clusters on the windowsill. One. It turns into solid streaks of rain, beating over everything on the other side of the glass. She moves away from the window, and stands in the middle of the room, where it is least dark.

There is a corner by the fireplace in this room where the wall is not quite straight. One side of the wall by the mantel nips in and out of a perfect right angle and then runs flush towards the door. The other slants a little down and out, and then bends back into a deep, tight, odd corner by the fireplace.

This is one of the few parts in the flat she's always thought might be a possible Place. She noticed it on the second visit, with the estate agent in tow. When he was out of the room taking a phone call, she used those few seconds of grace to bob down, and stretch her fingers tentatively into the corner. One, two, three. Her nails scraped against wood and paint.

Even so, maybe she should try again now. There seems to be a magic and a darkness in this storm that throws stronger shadows. Perhaps it would be enough to get her through. She comes to kneel at the side of the fireplace, and looks into the corner, hesitates.

And then, in a pause between lightning and thunder, another, closer, peal. The doorbell. She freezes, and then scrambles up, stopping, for a second, to see herself reflected in the mirror over the mantelpiece, a shadow-eyed woman, inside a room alone. The bell peals out again.

The blue of his shirt is dark with water, stuck to his skin, wet fabric tight around the curve of his shoulders and chest. He has taken his glasses off and holds them in his hand, and his eyes are larger and greener behind the wet clumps of lashes. The rain has gathered the tuft of hair over his forehead into one pointed curve, sending an endless procession of drops down his face. He is unexpected, unfamiliar, unknown all over again.

For a moment she stares at him. What are you doing here?

I don't know, he says.

She steps back to let him into the house. They are silent as they climb the stairs, and it is not until they are inside her front door that she lets herself speak.

I wasn't expecting you, today.

I know, he says. I wasn't expecting me, either. I just had to see you.

They are still standing up. Now that they are inside, he seems to look even wetter.

You're soaked, she says.

I had to park the car three streets away. I didn't have a coat. I didn't think. I just left.

Left?

No, not like that, he says quickly. Or maybe it is. I don't know.

She focuses on the practicalities, the things she can see in front of her. You need dry clothes, she says. I need to find you something.

He has never left a single thing here, apart from a clear plastic toothbrush that could be anyone's. Even after all these visits, he is always careful to repack his suitcase exactly as it was before he arrived.

He runs his hand back through his hair, sending a new

succession of drops down his back. Yes, I could do with drying off, he says. If you don't mind.

He tries to smile at her, but she only catches the very beginning of it, turning away before she will feel forced to return it. She hides her face in the shelves of her wardrobe and thinks only about the size of his body, the size of the clothes she has to give him.

There's this, she says, pulling out a big, faded sweatshirt. This might fit, perhaps. And a bathrobe.

A towel too, please, if you have one handy. He has come round to stand behind her, and touches her gently on one shoulder. She can smell the wetness on his skin. She tries to stay still, tries not to twist away, and presses the plump folds of the towel gently between them.

Here, she says. Give me your wet clothes. I'll hang them out. Or I can put the heating on? Then they'll be dry in an hour.

As soon as she has said this, she wishes she hadn't. They have no pattern for this day, no set routine, no alarm clock that tells them when, exactly, he will leave her again. She looks up at him, and the frown of his forehead shows he does not know the answer either.

It's actually got a bit chilly, she says. I think I'll put the heating on anyway.

Soon his clothes are draped over the radiators, the fabric drying in crisping lines, and he is sitting on her sofa, in a bundle of cotton and towelling, his hair tousled and curling as it dries. It is so at odds with the way he normally looks there, leaning back in a pair of suit trousers and a smart shirt, that it is then she manages to smile as she sits down beside him.

You're quite the sight.

I'm sorry, he says. I feel such an idiot.

I thought you'd be at home today, she says. Not here.

He sighs and sits back, pulling the towelling closer over his legs. I was, he says. I should be. But Harriet went back up north yesterday, and it was just us, and I suddenly knew I couldn't be there any more. Anna had gone out to town. I wrote her a note about a work emergency and I just – left.

A work emergency, she says.

I just wanted to be with you, and I panicked. I didn't know how else to do it.

He sits up again, turning towards her, reaching out one hand for her knee. I don't normally do things like this. I don't want to do things like this.

It's not ideal, no, she says. You're lucky I was in.

I'm sorry, he says again, his hand heavy on her knee. I didn't mean to land on you like this. I didn't mean for this to happen at all.

I don't think either of us did, she says.

Shit, he says. The two of them sit side by side, and stare at the fireplace.

Outside, the rain has settled into a steady, pattering fall. The gloom is gradually fading into dark.

I'll stay until it stops, anyway, he says. If that's all right.

Of course it is, she says. Although she is not completely sure that this is the case.

There is another pause. The rain drips down a gutter outside the window.

It is wonderful to see you, you know, he says. I was thinking about you. All weekend, I couldn't stop thinking about you.

Me too, she says.

Did you have a good time? With your mum?

For some reason, she does not tell him about their discussion. I helped her weed the garden, she says. And we drank tea. A lot of tea.

He laughs. Me too. Harriet was over for most of the weekend, with Meredith. Lovely girl. They're pretty serious. Anna thinks they might get married. Which she's pleased about. Though she's nervous about the idea of planning a lesbian wedding. She—

He stops himself. Anyway, he says then, it was nice to see Harriet. I don't get to see much of her, these days. But she seems very happy.

Does Harriet talk about Tom? she asks, to keep the conversation going. It is something she has been wondering for a while.

He shakes his head. She never talks about him, he says, but then none of us do, not really. I'm sure she must think about him though.

Of course she must, she says.

I know you only knew them right at the end, but they were so close as little children. They were always off, doing things together, playing these great, involved games. I'd often go into one of their rooms to check on them at night, and find them both together, wrapped around each other in the one bed. I'd have to prise them apart.

I'm glad she's happy, she says.

It's a relief, he admits. She was so angry as a teenager, all those haircuts and piercings and late nights and god knows what else. Although, we sort of put that down to, you know, Tom, as much as anything else. But she seems to have sorted herself out.

There is another silence, and she can put the question off no longer.

It looks like the rain is stopping, she says. What do you want to do?

They do not even manage to make it off the sofa and into the bedroom. At first, she pulls back a little as his lips meet hers. A bright, outer part of her, that seems to lace every muscle and tendon, knows this was inevitable, that this is what she and he have both wanted since he first entered the house, that they have bodies that are meant to be grasped and pressed together, chest to chest. She needs this, she needs him. It could not have happened any other way.

But all the same, there is a narrow but sure passage of darkness in her, somewhere deep under her breastbone, that takes her by surprise with the certainty of knowing it does not want to be touched and held and constricted by this, by him. It is a small space, cold and black and strung with reflections and words and occasionally a corner that expands past itself and flickers out of the bone. She pushes these flickers back down and tries to let her hands and her arms and her hips take over. She presses her face to his hair. It is still slightly damp and smells of outdoors, of storm and earth and sunshine and sweat. She breathes in all of these things and holds them in her lungs until they beat back the darkness.

I want you, he says at some point, not that much later on. I want you so much.

I want you too, she lets her voice say, and it is only half a lie.

Is it possible then, she thinks, to want, and to *not want*, at the same time? She looks up and holds the odd corner of the chimneybreast in her eyeline, daring it to move, to change, and let the darkness climb out and take her into it.

It does not, of course it does not. But maybe that is not

the point. None of this can actually ever lead her back to the Places, or further away from them either. And if this is true, then why are they here now, with the wanting and the not-wanting of their bodies holding them together on this sofa? She looks back down to him and closes her eyes.

They both sleep afterwards, for a little while, curled into each other along the length of the sofa, and when she wakes it is dark. He is leaning down to check his phone, a vivid blue square under his hand. It's late, he says. Eight o'clock.

His finger is moving, tapping hesitantly over the light.

What are you doing? she says.

Just sending a text, he says. Sorry. I'll be done in a minute.

It is to Anna, she realises, of course it is to Anna. The work emergency is more serious than he thought, don't wait up, he'll be home very late or even, in fact, he's been put up for the night and will see her tomorrow. Fascinated, she sits up and pulls his discarded towelling robe around herself, watching him create the story, tap by tap. She has never been so close to the lie before. It is more than a minute before he finishes. It is a long, long message, and right at the end, she glimpses a double kiss.

Sorry about that, he says. She reaches over to switch on the table lamp, and then draws her hand back again. This is something that might be said more easily in the dark.

You should go, she says.

He moves himself back up and nearer, unsteadying the sofa under her. It's all right, he says. I've said I won't be back tonight.

No, she says. I think you should go anyway. Properly go. Clare?

She presses her knees up under her chin, and looks at the outline of him, of the head and shoulders and arms and legs she has come to know so well. This was never a good idea, she manages. You know that as well as I do.

Darling, he says. Please. No. I love being here. I love being with you.

But what for? she says. Why are we doing this?

Do you want me to leave Anna? Because I can. I will. If you want me to.

She scrambles off the sofa, away from him. No, she says, no, I don't want you to leave Anna for me. I'm not sure I even want you to *have left* Anna. I want—' And there she stops, because she is not sure of what she wants, at all. A flicker escapes from the black place in her chest and comes rising up as a dark, rippling sob.

Oh Clare, he says, and he is up too, moving his arms around her, whispering into her ear as if it were a seashell. Look, he is saying, I know this isn't ideal. We've both always known that. But you are the most precious thing to me. I can't lose you. I don't know what I'd do without you now. Please don't do this. Please don't. Please.

But it's not right, she tries again, into his shoulder. None of this. None of this is right.

There are lots of things in this world that aren't right, he says, even more quietly. But we just have to make the best of them.

They stand together, in the darkness, in the middle of a room that they cannot see. He presses his hand to her cheek.

He's all we ever talk about, you know, she says. Him, and the Places. I can't help thinking, that if he was still here, we would never have done this. Been this.

We can't second-guess that, he says, with a faint echo of his usual, pragmatic tone.

But it's true.

I do like talking about him with you, yes, he admits. That bit is true enough. But I didn't think you minded. And that's not why I love you.

Isn't it?

Look, he says, Tom or no Tom, I want to be with you now, in *this* place, not any other. And I'll do whatever it takes to make it right. I promise.

She pulls herself back out of the circle of his arms, and tightens the robe around herself before switching on the lamp. He clicks into tired life in front of her, staring at her with dark water in his eyes, exactly as if she is the coast-guard giving him that news, all over again.

I'm sorry, she says. I do love you, I do.

He sighs. The lines on his face look deeper than they ever have before. He is suddenly old and hard. Then what do you want me to do? You say you still love me. You say you don't want to carry on like this. But you say you don't want me to leave Anna. So what am I meant to do, Clare? Tell me that.

You can't do anything. She cannot control the tears rising in her eyes, and starts to cry again. It's just not right. Not just because of Anna. Because of Tom. Because of all that.

Tom isn't part of this relationship.

Isn't he? she says. Could you say right now, truthfully, we could never, ever, talk about him again and still stay together?

He's my son, he says quietly.

She wipes a hand over her wet cheeks and tries again. I didn't mean – I didn't mean we could never talk about him. I just meant maybe we shouldn't be together just because of it. That it's better this way.

It's never going to be better this way. Or any other way.

But I don't know that, she says. Not for sure.

This is it, Clare. This is the real world. Trust me, this is all there is.

He does not look at her as he goes over to the radiator, pulling each piece of clothing off it with a sharp tug. A shirt, a sock, a pair of trousers. Another sock. She watches him gather his belongings, try to reassemble himself into the person he was before he came here.

So, that's it then? he says. I leave now, and never speak to you again?

She feels the first flare of panic at the thought of never hearing from him, never knowing where he is, what he is feeling, but that deep inky place inside her makes her say well, perhaps it's for the best if you don't. For now.

Fine, he says again. Fine. He straightens his shirt collar with one final, abrupt pull.

Look, I'm really sorry, she tries, I truly am.

He cuts her off, and walks down the stairs towards the door. Let's not bother talking about this any more. If you've decided. I mean, what the hell is the point?

There are no right words to say. From above, she watches him open the door and start to disappear in the frame of the doorway.

Wait, she says suddenly, too loudly, wait, please. I just want you to know I never minded. About the talking, I mean. I never minded at all.

He turns inside the frame to consider her, and then gives a small, terrible laugh. Thank you, he says shortly. He starts to step through the door again, and then hesitates. Oh god, your bloody Places, Clare, he says, into the hollow of the hallway, you and your bloody Places! You know, I wish now you'd never told me.

And then he closes the door on himself.

It is not until after she hears the street door slam that she allows herself to sit just where she is on the stairs, and be still. She is alone again, with the darkness plucking at her from the corners. Her hands, her feet, her chest are frosted over with black. Her face flames up where his fingers have rested on her cheekbone, and then after a little while, goes out.

*

1995

The storm went on all night, with a wind that gusted through the cracks in the window, and threw rain spattering against the panes. It was so loud that Clare got up to peer out of the window, but all she could see was the shadows of the trees at the bottom of the garden tossing back and forth in the sky, behind the streaks of rain running down the glass.

There was movement in the bed behind her. 'Bug?' Josie whispered. 'Are you all right?'

Clare started. 'I'm fine,' she said. 'I just wanted to see the storm.'

In a rustle of sheets, Josie was up, tiptoeing over to stand beside her. 'Pretty wild out there, eh? You're not scared?'

'Not now,' Clare said.

Josie put her arm around Clare's shoulder, and they watched the black trees jostle against the clouds. 'It must be coming off the sea,' Josie murmured. 'That's why it's so windy. A proper sea storm. Just like we used to get, eh?'

Clare looked up at her, questioning. 'Oh, you won't remember, I suppose. The Scarborough flat. You know, where we lived when you were very little, near Nan's.'

'I don't think I do,' Clare said, but she thought of a red

wall painted with giraffes, and a long, dark flight of stairs, with a coarse woven carpet that scraped along her knees. 'Maybe, a bit.'

'It was tiny,' Josie said, laughing, 'but then again, you didn't take up much space. Still don't, really.'

A new cluster of raindrops smacked against the window. 'It was right at the top, our little flat,' Josie said. 'Just you and me. When the storms came in, you really felt them, up there.'

'Like this?' Clare said.

Josie put her other hand on Clare's other shoulder. 'No,' she said. 'Not like this at all.'

It was quiet by morning. Clare and Josie both slept in a little later than normal, and when Clare woke up, it was to a grey, dripping, defeated world. The big trees looked bowed over, and the fence down one side of the lawn had been pulled down, slats spilling over the grass.

'Oh dear,' Josie said. 'We'd better tell the owners about that. I'll mention it to the others at breakfast.'

But when they came downstairs, the only person up was Tom, stirring a spoon around in a murky bowl of disintegrating Coco Pops. 'They're all still asleep,' he said. 'Although Harri is just pretending, I think.'

'Well, it was a late night for all of us, I suppose,' Josie said. 'And it's not like they're missing out on any sunshine.' She flicked on the kettle.

'We can still go out today, though, can't we?' Tom said, stirring faster. 'Dad promised we'd go to the beach today.'

'It's not exactly beach weather,' Josie said.

Tom's eyes became darker. 'It was a promise,' he said fiercely, into the bowl. 'He promised.'

Josie blinked and paused for a moment, hand on the

kettle. 'Well, let's wait and see what your dad says, when he's up, shall we? Clare, do you want toast or cereal?'

Clare had known there would be an argument about it, ever since the first moment Tom had mentioned it in the kitchen. It was not the sort of day where it was going to be easy to convince anyone to go to the beach, and it was definitely not the sort of day to be fighting about it. But Tom didn't seem to feel the same.

'But you promised,' he kept saying. 'I don't see why we shouldn't go.'

'Because it's pissing down with rain, you moron.'

'*Language*, Harriet.'

'And nobody goes to the beach on a rainy day. Except weirdos.'

'Shut up! It's not fair!'

She understood why he was upset. The more you sensed the Places, the more you wanted to be near them, to get as close to, as far inside them as you as could. Tom was more sensitive to them than she was, she knew that, but she still felt it.

And it seemed like, apart from that one they'd found in the mirrors, all the others big enough for them to get through seemed to be on the coast, in the darkness and the reflections of the water and the caves. So that's where they needed to go. Maybe that's it, she thought, maybe they need the right sort of darkness, the right sort of reflection. Maybe that's what can create them. Pleased, she stored this thought away, to write down and to tell Tom later, when the argument was over.

'Hey,' Marcus said, 'hey, guys. Harriet, stay out of it.' He came round to his son. Tom was up on his feet, his thin arms bent and fingers clenched into angry pink-white shells. 'Look, buddy, it's not a great day today. And yes, I know, I promised, but it's not going to be much fun when it's not sunny, is it?'

'That doesn't matter,' Tom said, through a tight strip of a mouth. 'That's not the *point*.' He seemed close to tears.

Marcus sighed. 'Is it that important to you?'

Tom nodded, looking down at the table in front of him. Clare watched.

'All right,' Marcus said. 'All right.' Tom raised his head, quickly, his eyes darting to his father's face.

'But, *Dad*!'

'Harriet, stay out of it! I hadn't finished.' He looked up from Tom, and around the table, from Harriet, crossly kicked back in her chair, past Clare and Josie, nursing her mug of tea, to Anna, perched against the cabinet, arms folded and coffee untouched on the side. 'Look, how about I take Tom to the cove down there now for a quick walk? The one just down the road? We can be down and back in an hour.'

'I think it's a great idea,' Harriet said. 'Maybe you could just leave him there.'

'*Harriet*,' Anna muttered, but the words came out too slowly, almost mechanically.

'And you, darling,' Marcus said, 'is that all right with you?'

Everyone looked at Anna. She shrugged, pulling one hand up and through her hair. 'Whatever you like, Marcus. Whatever you like.'

'Well,' Marcus said, 'why don't you go off and get your stuff together then, Tom?' He did not look at Anna as he said it.

Tom was suddenly all white, bright smiles and swinging arms. He slipped away from the table and beyond, into his bedroom.

'Well, thank god for that,' Harriet said. Josie stood up and began to gather together plates and cups and bowls. The storm had passed over, it was dying away.

'Could I go to the beach too?' Clare said. She was really asking Josie, but she looked at Marcus.

Marcus raised his eyebrows behind his glasses. 'Of course you can, if you want to. If that's all right with you, Josie.'

Josie shook her head at her. 'Do what you like, Clare. Do exactly what you like.' For a second, she sounded just like Anna.

Clare did not feel very good about leaving Josie there in the storm-damaged house with Anna and Harriet. 'Why don't you come too?' she said, as Josie was helping her find her shoes, her hairband, her jacket.

'I don't think that would be a very good idea, do you?' Josie said, and then stopped herself. 'Forget I said that.'

'Why not?' Clare persisted, but Josie wouldn't say anything else.

'Just you forget about that and go off and have a nice walk, and come back and tell me all about it later, eh?'

'Will you ask them to fix the fence?' Clare said. She looked out again at it, at the sturdy strips of wood sprawled over the grass.

Josie laughed, a proper laugh. 'Yes, we'll get the fence fixed. I promise. Now go on with you.'

They all, by some mutual, unspoken agreement, started to walk very fast as soon as they got out of the gate, and on to the road beyond. The road sloped down towards the coast, flanked on both sides by a row of little houses. A lot of them were lived in by holidaymakers too, you could tell. There were yellow and blue plastic buckets and spades tipped over on some of the patios, and on one house, wet beach towels with cartoon characters on them clung, dripping, to railings.

'Oops. They're lucky they didn't lose those last night,' Marcus said.

'Oops,' Tom echoed, cheerfully. Clare smiled at him. He was fizzing with the same intent glow that she had seen on the first day.

The road tapered, at the end, into a smaller path, with gorse stretching up on both sides to form a green, prickly tunnel. Marcus had to stoop slightly, in parts, while Tom and Clare ran on ahead.

When they came out of the tunnel, they were on the cliff path, looking down over a drop of steep rocks and steps at a small curve of sand that formed a little bay, a grey sea breaking up and on to it. It looked very similar to the beach they had been to on that first day.

'Tide's in,' Marcus said, coming up behind them, 'but looks like there's still enough sand to go down on to it. Shall we?'

There were a lot of steps to climb down. It was slippy in places, with sandy pools of water sitting in the dip of some of the treads and it was still windy out here, on the cliff edge. Pieces of hair kept falling out of her ponytail and whipping across her mouth. 'Go carefully now,' Marcus told them, and Clare was careful, although Tom raced ahead. He seemed to know exactly where to put each foot, while she had to grip the rail and come down steadily, step after step. Marcus followed her. 'Take your time,' he said, close behind her. 'I'll wait for you.'

When they finally reached the beach, Tom was already moving across it, away from them, pacing the grey-yellow sand out around the rocks and cliff edges. 'Catch up with him, Clare, go on,' Marcus said, and dizzy with wind and sea and sand, she ran off, away from Marcus, to join the skinny, dark-haired figure, picking his way intently from rock to rock.

'So,' she said, breathing heavily, 'what do you think? Is there anything?'

Tom hopped off the rock he had been standing on. 'Let's just be still for a moment,' he suggested. 'See if we can feel anything.'

They faced each other, and he closed his eyes, so Clare did the same. She felt wind skating across her cheeks, her hair flicking across her eyelids, the sea crashing and breaking behind her. And then, a quiver of something else, more tremulous, less definite, darker. Before she could stop herself, she cried out and opened her eyes again.

Tom nodded, pleased. 'I thought so. It's there, somewhere.'

He had become still and steady again, a cat scenting out his prey, just like the panthers they'd watched on a nature documentary the other night. He started to stalk away from her again, and Clare followed him, trying to imitate his pace, his steps, his movements. 'It must be around here,' he said to her, over his shoulder. 'It's this side, isn't it?'

Clare stopped and considered. There was a tingling *pull* on the left side of the cliff in the bay, as if something was clutching at her with a thousand tiny black needle-like fingers, at the same time as trying to push her away again. 'Yes,' she said. 'Definitely.'

'Good,' Tom said, and they carried on, zigzagging in and out of every rocky outcrop. Clare glanced back. Marcus was just a small figure sitting on a rock near the foot of the steps, one leg crossed over the other knee, resting an open book on his shin.

'It's not here,' Tom said. 'Why isn't it here?' He stood and looked up at the cliff. 'Unless it's up there?'

When Clare looked up, the feeling did not become any stronger. 'I don't think so, do you?' she said. 'It doesn't feel like it, to me.'

They had reached the sea's edge. They could go no further along the rocks. Tom stood for a moment, shoulders hunched, and examined the rocks where the water broke over them in foamy splashes. 'Nothing for it, I suppose,' he said, 'but to go back.'

'We could try again later,' Clare said. 'When the tide's down.'

Tom shook his head. 'I'm not sure, you know, that it's any further out along that cliff either. It feels nearer than that. Maybe even inside the cliff, where we can't get to it. Just not *here*.' He dismissed the rock face with one dejected hand.

'You want to go back, already?' Marcus said, as they came towards him. 'Really? Well, okay.'

Tom's head had dropped. All the white-hot energy in his body from earlier had completely vanished. 'Never mind,' Marcus said, attempting to put an arm around him. 'We'll come back, when it's sunny. It'll be more fun, you know, when it's sunny.'

'I don't know,' Tom said. He walked away from Marcus and began to climb the steps.

Marcus looked back at Clare. 'Blew a few cobwebs away, at least.'

Clare smiled for him and nodded.

They climbed back up the cliff a lot more slowly than they had come down it. When they reached the top of the steps, Marcus insisted they stop and look back at the sea.

'Clouds or no clouds,' he said, 'it's still a beautiful view. Look at that. Magic.'

Clare turned to look at the sea, the clouds, the jagged points of the cliffs curving round them. 'It's beautiful,' she said.

'It is, isn't it? Hey, hang on,' Marcus said, suddenly sharper, 'Tom, buddy, where are you going? Keep to the path!'

Tom had started to run away from them along the cliff, his black head flicking in and out of the gorse. His voice came blowing back. 'It's all right! I'm on the path!'

'Stay here, Clare, a second,' Marcus said, and he followed his son down into the scrubby bushes.

As soon as she stood there alone and closed her eyes, she knew why Tom had run off. There was that strange trembling again, pulling at her. Even though Marcus had told her to stay where she was, she followed it, steady step after steady step.

She came upon them both a few minutes later, standing in a place where the gorse parted to show another rocky curve just along from the bay they'd been standing in earlier. This one reached out further from the land, and here there was no sand. The high water crashed up deep against the rocks. The trembles seized her spine. 'It's another beach,' Tom said to her, thrilled.

'Or it will be, at low tide,' Marcus said.

'Could we get down to it, do you think?' she asked, trying not to sound too excited.

Marcus peered over towards the other bay. 'There's no steps, but looks like we could walk round from that first one, when the sea's out. Could be fun. Probably some good rock pools and caves down there too.'

'Caves,' Tom said. 'Caves.'

Everything in Clare shivered. She did not know what to say, so she looked up again, and out over the cliffs. There was a point on the horizon where grey sea met grey cloud, and you could not tell them apart.

9

The Darkest Tower

She has to keep going to work, of course. People do. She has to keep going to work, and coming home again, and going to the supermarket to buy things to eat, and replacing the soap when it runs out, and putting clothes in the washing machine early enough in the evening that it isn't going to disturb Lilian downstairs, and opening gas bills, and paying them, and filling Tupperware pots full of leftovers to take to the office for lunch tomorrow, and plugging in her phone to charge it, and hanging out clothes to dry, and then putting them away again, and remembering, for god's sake, to always close the window before leaving for work so that next door's cigarette smoke doesn't drift in and make her coats smell.

There are so many little things that take up a day. She has somehow never noticed the smallness or frequency of them before. It seems they are always there – as soon as one is done, there are ten others jostling to be remembered and completed. They have always been there, haven't they? And yet now, they seem to be teasing her into these strange, frustrating cycles of doing and then using and then redoing, just to use and redo all over again. It seems pointless, somehow, in a way she cannot quite explain.

She has not told Josie yet. Her mother has not called, and she has not called her, either. She knows Josie will be pleased about the break-up, and this makes her want to tell her less. She comes home and switches her phone to silent, and then focuses on these tiny circles she traces from bedroom to bathroom to kitchen and back again.

Maybe it is better that she has these little things. Because if she did not have them, she would have nothing at all.

She sleeps. This is one thing she can remember how to do, and she is relieved to discover she can still do it well. She is tired all the time. The moment where she stoops to sit on the edge of her bed, lifting her feet away from the floor and gathering the covers up around her, is the best part of each evening. This day is over, it is done. It can expect nothing more from her now. She closes her eyes into the soft, white roughness of the sheets and lets herself float up into them and disappear.

She dreams.

It seems obvious to expect that she would dream about him, but she does not. Instead, it is Tom who sails with her into most of these nights adrift. Sometimes she is with him, back on the island, and they are both small again, on beaches so bright that the light squeezes her eyes, and sometimes they are dragged through into the darkness, the sun fading into tiny petrol-spill pinpricks around them. Sometimes Tom speaks words that she remembers him saying, and sometimes he talks about events and places that he could never have known, and sometimes he will not speak at all, and she only knows he is there by the grip of the bones of his fingers on her own. And there are some nights where she thinks she wakes up here in this place, and goes out into the hall to find that crack of the stair splitting wider into the lost, trembling blackness, and she hears his voice, and puts her hand down on to the carpet and *through*.

Out of all of them, she hates waking up from these dreams the most.

I'm busy, she tells Josie, occasionally. Just busy. Work and stuff. Let's talk more soon.

All right, Josie says. Soon.

Her mother has been even more abrupt than usual on the phone since that weekend at home, and for once, she is grateful. Josie is afraid to hear anything about him. And she is afraid to tell her. It is the perfect arrangement.

She puts one day on top of another day on top of another day, until she is no longer sure how many days it has been since he left for the last time. Is it even appropriate to measure the time in days any more, when it is building up into such a tall tower? Occasionally she is bold enough to start to stack it out in weeks. Sometimes she can only manage the hours.

She starts to feel as if her skin is becoming thinner, the veins beneath darker and more pronounced. She has stopped seeing herself in the mirror. The only time she looks at her body now is through her eyes alone, dissected into pieces. A rested arm on a knee, a foot in a shoe to be laced, a pair of chapped hands washing a cup, strands of hair peppering a pale shoulder, a freckled breast lifting slightly against jersey cotton as she pulls a T-shirt up and over her head. None of these things seems to belong to her any more. She turns over the arm of this stranger, and traces the new dark lines up from the wrist with somebody else's fingers.

Are you all right? her friend Meena asks her, some time after she has stopped counting the days. An evening meal that she could not work out how to cancel, a vase with a single gerbera, white plates of pasta and a bottle of house red that tastes acid against the back of her throat.

I mean, Meena says, you've been quiet. More quiet than usual, anyway. And you look, well, a bit tired. Sorry.

I'm fine, she says. And then that strange, dark honesty that pulled itself out of her the last few weeks compels her to add, well, sort of.

Sort of?

It's just sort of been a difficult time.

Meena spears a couple of tiny, curled shells on her fork. Okay, look, stop saying sort of, she says. It's clearly more than that. What's wrong?

It does not seem the right place to begin an explanation of something that is already over. But she has nobody but herself to blame for that.

I was seeing someone, she says. And then we broke up.

She manages to say it quite calmly, concentrating on chasing a smeared strand of pasta towards the rim of the plate and trapping it there, against the flat of her knife.

Wow, Meena says, wow. She has dropped her fork. What, like really seeing someone? I mean, you never see people, do you? Clare, that's big.

I know, she says. It was big. But now it's over. So.

Meena's brown eyes are wide in her face. I can't believe you didn't tell me, she says. I mean, who is he? How did you meet him? And oh, I'm so sorry it's over. What happened? Are you very upset?

It's complicated, she says. It's a bit hard to explain.

Were you in love? Start from the beginning, Meena says. Start from the beginning and tell me absolutely *everything*.

She tells her *most* things.

Somehow, telling Meena about him and their relationship, hearing the words come out of the mouth she knows to be her own, makes her feel like the story starts to belong to her. These last unexpected months actually happened to her, and to him too.

She lets herself, for the first time, think about what he might be doing. Has he let himself sink into a pool of chores and tasks and numbered days too? She doubts it. Like her, he has gone home to the life he lived before. Maybe he went back to Anna that night, and turned to her as she switched out the light, pulling her into an embrace he had half-forgotten, discovering a body to replace the one that she has taken away from him. She shudders, despite herself.

But no, it is good for her to remember that although this happened, to both of them, there is a whole other life that has happened to him too, for far longer than anything that was between them, a whole life of marriage, and joint mortgage agreements and birth certificates and an endless procession of family meals around a table. That was his life, and this here is hers. She must continue to live this one that she has always had, and try not to think that it had been ever different. Maybe everything has happened exactly as it should.

It is then she remembers something that hasn't happened exactly as it should.

The two blue lines are very clear. She'll go to the doctor, of course, just to be sure, because isn't that what you do, just to be sure, but in a way she feels she doesn't need to be any more certain than she is now. She thinks about the last time she was with him, in a hazy, unexpected confusion of towelling and sofa cushions and the smell of damp cloth steaming on the radiators. Neither of them had been prepared for that day. And deep inside the certainty, she is sure of this too: neither of them is prepared for this day either.

She traces the lattice of veins down her arm again. They are warm and raised, bulging slightly under the pressure of her fingers. Inside, the blood pulses through them, moving through her body and down, eventually, into that little dark cluster of cells.

*

1995

'Be careful now, it's slippy,' Anna said, as they climbed down the steps and on to the slick wet cobbles of the causeway. The stones stretched out in front of them, curved square pressed against curved square, on and on towards a black, rocky outcrop in the distance.

'That's Lihou there,' Marcus said, pointing to it. 'When the tide's up, all this is under water. The house on that island's completely cut off.'

'But do they have a boat?' Clare asked.

'You probably wouldn't bother with one,' Anna said. 'I expect, if you lived there, you'd just wait until the water went down again.' She started to walk down the causeway, stepping around the trickles of seawater running between the stones, and Josie and Harriet followed her.

'It would be like having a moat round a castle,' Clare said. 'A giant moat. To keep people out.'

Tom smiled at her. 'That would be good.'

'Come on then,' Marcus said. 'We've got a tide to beat, after all.'

The causeway guided them all the way to the little island, between sharp rocks studded with thick wigs of seaweed and pools of sandy, rippling water. 'Stick to the path,' Anna cautioned the children, and Clare obeyed. She felt no inclination to step off the reassuringly straight line of stones. However, as they walked along, Tom wavered on the very edge of the cobbles, occasionally slipping off the path to nudge a clump of weed with the toe of his shoe, or to stoop to feel the ridge of a limpet shell glued to a rock.

'Tom,' Anna kept saying, 'what did I say now? Tom?'

'It's all right,' Marcus said. 'I'm keeping an eye on him, darling. Don't worry.'

Anna stopped walking, and fixed Marcus with a wary, wide-eyed look. 'Well, *you* can be the one who carries him home when he slips and breaks his ankle, then.'

'Darling,' Marcus said, again. Behind him, Tom stood on the ridge of a rock, his arms splayed in perfectly balanced stillness.

'What's there to see on this island, then?' Josie said, stepping closer to Anna. 'What's actually out there?'

Anna turned her head. 'Well,' she said, 'it's a funny little place, really ...'

And suddenly they were all moving on and towards the island again, passing through the dark, jagged rocks, and finally up on to a grey shingle beach.

The house was at the top of the beach, half-hidden behind a mottled wall. In its long black roof was set a row of blank windows, and a thick, sloping chimney. It seemed to be quietly, patiently waiting for them, here in this land of rock and wiry, salt-swept shrubs. They stumbled over the shingle towards it, the stones clicking together under their feet.

'Can you imagine what it would be like to live here?' Josie said.

'It doesn't look like anyone does,' Clare said. 'It's so quiet, isn't it?'

They all looked at the house, and the house looked back.

On the other side of the island, facing out over the sea, they came across a set of low, crumbling stone walls arranged in rectangles, showing where rooms and doorways had once been. A couple of sheep nudged their way along one ruined edge, and down below them, waves crashed against rocks.

'The old priory,' Marcus told them. 'Where the monks used to live, in medieval times.'

In one wall, the old bricks still reached up to form an arch, leading to a narrow, dark alcove. As soon as he spotted it, Tom went over to it, slipping under the wooden barrier in the archway.

Clare followed him up to the barrier, leaning over it to see better into the gloom. Tom was still wholly there, running his fingers over the walls with fidgety frustration. 'It's just normal,' he said. 'All of it, just normal.'

It felt like exactly the sort of structure where something should be, and yet there did not seem to be anything there at all. It was a disappointment.

'You better come out then,' Clare said, 'before the parents see. I don't think we're supposed to go in there.'

'There's only one place I'm *supposed* to go,' Tom muttered, ducking back under the plank. 'I just wish they'd let me.'

'We'll get to go back down to that beach before the end of the holiday, I'm sure,' Clare said.

Tom rose up and faced her. A red spot dotted the sharpness of each cheekbone. 'Are you?' he said. 'I'm not.' He started to walk away, back towards the picnic table where

Anna and Josie were pulling sandwiches and cans out of their rucksacks.

'Come on, Clare,' Josie called. 'Aren't you hungry?'

As Clare made her way over to them, something sea-pink and bright made her look down and into the crack of one of the ruined walls. She knelt down and prised it out. It was a flat, smooth grey stone, the size of both her palms. On it, somebody had painted a wreath of pink and white flowers with green leaves, encircling white letters that spelt out 'Lihou Island Treasure Stone'.

She could not speak for a moment with the surprise of it. What did it mean? Why was it here? Cupping the Treasure Stone in her hands, she stood up again and carried on towards the picnic table.

'What have you got there?' Marcus said, and dumbstruck, she opened her hands to show him. 'Hey, Clare's found a Treasure Stone!'

They all crowded around her, except for Tom, who stayed sitting on the bench, biting into his sandwich. 'What's that?' Josie said. 'What is it?'

'The people who live in that house back there,' Harriet said, 'they do this totally weird thing where they make them and hide them in places on the island.'

'Such fun for the kids,' Anna said. 'Harriet found one once, didn't you?'

Harriet shrugged. 'Yeah, when I was like, seven.'

'So I can keep it?' Clare said.

'Finders keepers,' Marcus said. 'As far as these go, anyway. It's yours.'

'Can I see?' Josie took the stone in her thin fingers and examined the delicate pink flowers closely. 'It must have taken so much time to do. I wonder how many of these they make,' she said. She looked up from the stone and smiled at Clare, a small, brittle curve of a smile. 'It's a beautiful, magic thing, bug. And to think you were the one who found it.'

After they had made a full circuit of the island, and the black roof of the house was in view again, Marcus led them down from the path and on to the shore. With the Treasure Stone safely zipped in her pocket, Clare hopped from rock to rock, the sharp edges making the rubber soles of her shoes bend and buckle. In front of her, Tom picked his way down.

'Look into this pool, you two,' Marcus said, crouching down by a dip in the rocks where seawater had collected. 'What can you see?'

They knelt down next to him, putting their hands on the gritty stone and leaning over, staring into the water. For a second, Clare could only see their three faces, each a series of anxious, silver-dark ripples, before she blinked again and saw below them, into the depths of the pool. Seaweed billowed out from the rocky walls and far down, sand lay at the bottom.

'I don't see anything,' she said, 'except the seaweed.'

'Look again,' Marcus said. 'Look closely, right down there.'

Clare stared hard at the bottom of the pool. Suddenly, the sand seemed to flicker. It couldn't be. Was it really another one, here in the darkness of the water? She sprang back and sat on her heels. 'Oh!' she said. 'Is it?'

And did that mean Marcus knew about them too, then? If he did, then it was all going to be all right. He could take them to find them. He could protect them from Jem.

Tom grabbed her arm. 'No,' he said, insistently, 'no.' He gestured back down into the water. 'Look,' he said, faintly mocking. 'It's just fish. That's all.'

She saw them then, small shapes skating over the bottom of the rock pool, with speckled scales that made them almost invisible against the sand. 'Oh,' she said again, and she felt her cheeks flush hot with the embarrassment of it.

'Just fish,' Marcus said. 'Honestly, Tom. Don't you think it's incredible that they've evolved so well like this, so they can't be seen on the seabed?'

'Yes,' Clare said firmly, 'I do.' She said it for Marcus, not for Tom.

On their walk back to the top of the causeway, where the others stood waiting for them to begin the return crossing, Marcus stooped and picked up something bright from the ground. 'Hey,' he said, almost to himself, 'now, would you look at that?'

'What?' Tom said. 'What have you found?'

Marcus opened his hand. On his palm, along with a few dark grains, was an even circle of frosted green, about the size and thickness of a fifty-pence piece. Against his skin, it seemed to glow.

'What is that?' Clare said. She could not stop staring at it.

'It's seaglass,' Marcus said. 'Pieces of old green bottles, mainly. They get rubbed by the sea and the sand so that they get this sort of rough look.' He touched it gently with the finger of his other hand. 'I've never seen one quite this regular, though. It's a proper circle. A perfect piece of glass.'

'A *real* treasure stone,' Tom said.

Marcus smiled. 'It is, isn't it?' He gave the seaglass coin to Tom, who held it up with two fingers and stared at it against the light.

'Can I have it?' Tom asked, still squinting up at his hand.

'Of course you can, buddy,' Marcus said. 'If you want it.'

'It's like it was waiting for us here,' Tom said, tucking it away in his pocket. 'Just waiting for us to come along and find it.'

Out across the sand, the water approached.

When they were ready to go out the next morning, Tom was missing. It was Clare who spotted him in the garden, a pair of white legs and dark sandals dangling from a low branch over the grey stone wall at the very end of the garden, half-hidden under the dripping shadows of the trees above. 'Look,' she said, pointing out of the kitchen window.

'Oh for heaven's sake. Silly boy. I hope he doesn't fall,' Anna said.

'Run down and get him, would you, Clare?' Marcus asked her, and grateful to be released from that room full of tense, quiet adults, Clare slipped on her shoes and stepped out on to the patio.

She trod steadily over the grass, feeling the wet earth under each footstep soak through the canvas of her shoes. By the time she reached the trees, Tom had lifted himself up higher into the branches, where he sat staring down at her, clutching the trunk. His shorts and legs were wet and speckled with black spots of bark and dirt, and his hair was damp and roughed back, clumped together like the fur of one of her grandma's cats.

'Your dad wants you to come in,' she said. 'We're going to some chapel, I think.'

'I'm not coming in,' Tom said.

She came closer to the wall, leaning on the stone and craning up so she could see his face better. 'What's happened?' she asked. 'Is it—'

He shook his head in one swift, frantic movement. 'You'd better come up.'

'I don't think I can,' Clare said. 'I'm not very good at climbing.'

'It's easy,' Tom said. 'Come on. I'll help you if you get stuck.'

'Your legs are longer than mine,' Clare pointed out, but all the same, she was already scrambling for a foothold on the stones of the wall, pressing her hands into the gritty wetness of the stones and finding a place to put her toe, the side of her foot, her knee on the top.

She stood up on the uneven stones, using the trunk of the tree to steady herself. 'Come on. That branch there,' Tom told her. 'And then that one.'

Following Tom's impatient directions, she ended up astride the branch below him, leaning back against the trunk. Up here, they were completely enclosed in a tent of long branches woven with green leaves. The house had disappeared from view. Her legs swung from the branch, but her back was steady against the damp bark. She felt giddy and safe and secret.

'We're so high up,' she said. 'What were you going to tell me, then?'

Tom frowned. 'I saw *him*,' he whispered. 'I saw him. And he shouted at me.'

'What? When?' Clare said. 'Now? But how?'

Tom leaned down to her, gripping the trunk even more tightly. 'When Dad went back up to Mum this morning, I knew they'd be a while. They always are. So I went back down to the cliff.'

'You did?' Clare whispered. 'Without asking?' She was shocked.

'Of course I didn't ask,' Tom said scornfully. 'They never would have said yes. But I needed to go back and check something.'

'Was the tide out?' Clare said. 'Did you get down?'

'No,' Tom said. 'It was just like yesterday. But even so, I thought if I could get a bit closer to it out along the cliff, just to have a look, it would be good. And I did. I think there's really a cave down there, like Dad said. But then I met *him*.'

'Jem?' Clare said.

'Ssh!' Tom shifted on his branch, and the leaves shook around them, sending drops of water pattering down on to the wall below. 'Yes. Him. It's like he knew I'd be there. He was really angry. And he knew, Clare. He *knew*.'

She felt as if the damp chill of the bark was sinking into the bones of her back. 'About the one down there?'

'About all of it.'

'But how? What did he say?'

Tom did not answer her. He was talking faster and quieter now. 'See,' he was saying, 'I've worked it all out, you see. He's angry because he knows they're there, but he can't get into them. And he thinks if he follows us in, he might be able to. He's like us. Or he was like us. But then he got old.'

'What do you mean?' Clare said.

'I think grown-ups can't get in, Clare. But maybe they don't ever stop being able to notice them like we do, not really.'

She was trying to understand. 'So, you're saying that when he was our age, he could get in like we can?'

Tom nodded. 'Yes, I think that's it.'

'And so when we're old, we won't be able to either?'

Tom nodded again, more slowly. 'We'll end up just like Jem.'

There was a horrible, still moment, where the trees dripped over them, and Clare thought about becoming old, as old as Jem, and never being able to find her way through again. Did it always have to happen like that? Silently, she promised herself that she would never forget how to see the gaps, how to find her way through the dark corners that were less solid than the rest of the world.

'I can see how he must be angry,' she said. And then she tried again. 'But I don't understand. What did he say to you? How did you know?'

Tom sighed. 'I was on the cliff, looking over to see if I could see the cave better, and he came up and grabbed me by the arm. He said all sorts of stuff about it being dangerous, and did my mum know I was fooling around here, and lots of stuff like that. And I shouted at him to let me go and how it was none of his business, and then – and then – he said something like "You may think nobody knows, but I know all about your games, you know. The places you go, you and the little miss."'

'Me?' Clare said.

'I told you,' Tom said, 'he knows. And then he said some more stuff, right in my ear, about how he used to be young just like me, and it was easy to do stupid things, and I shouldn't think life would be like this forever. And then I finally got free and ran away, and he shouted after me. "Careful," he said, "I've got my eye on you. You and the little miss too."'

Clare wrapped her arms around her own goose-pimpled shoulders. 'Maybe we *should* tell Mum and your parents,' she said.

Tom looked down at her. 'It's no good. You know it's no good. All I know is we mustn't show him the way in. When we go into that one down there, it has to be in secret.'

'We can't until the tide's down, anyway,' Clare said. 'When does that happen?'

Tom dug his nails into the brown, soft bark. 'Well,' he said, 'it better be soon.'

And then Marcus's face was down far under their feet, asking if they were ready to go.

10

The Magician's Revenge

She is watching a black screen dotted with erratic flickers of white. A cold, hard pressure slides over and around on the skin of her abdomen, guided by a gloved hand above. She looks from the screen to the hand to the face above it, dark hair scraped back, a pair of tortoiseshell glasses resting on soft, sagging cheeks.

Look, the technician says, look, right there. She moves the instrument up and back and down again, and the image on the screen bulges, and the white clouds swim together to form a sudden, definite roundness there in the dark that surrounds it. That's the head, the technician says. Can you see it?

She stares at the circle and can say nothing. On the screen, it hovers, trembling.

The technician looks at her and smiles. Quite something, isn't it, seeing it for the first time like that?

She remembers herself, remembers the hand pressing on her skin. Yes, she manages, oh yes. It's just I hadn't expected it to be so clear.

Your baby's fully formed at this stage, the technician says. Hands, eyes, toes, the whole lot. And everything looks good here, from what I can see.

The technician slides the metal back and forth around her belly button again, and picks out for her, in grainy white focus, the legs, the arms, the head proudly upright on the torso.

And see that? the technician says, pointing to a pulsing dot, somewhere near the middle of the screen. That's your baby's heartbeat there. A good strong one too.

Oh, she says. Oh. She watches it send clear, regular flickers out into the dark.

So, nothing to worry about here at all, the doctor says in the consulting room. Everything looks perfectly normal. We'll see you at twenty weeks. And before she has time to think about it, she is out on the street again, in the middle of a working day, clutching a handful of papers and leaflets to her chest.

Really, she should go back to the office, but she finds her feet taking her away from the bus station, and weaving purposefully down through the bollards into the shopping precinct. As she walks, she cannot help but keep one hand resting on the fabric of her skirt, just below the waistband. Somewhere here, under the layers of cotton and skin and fat and tensing muscles, there really is a person with a head and arms and legs, and a frantic, beating miniature heart. She has been able to spy on them, through that screen, floating into existence there in their darkened, dolls' house world. They are real.

Of course, she has thought about an abortion. The word goes hand in hand with missed periods, and furtively bought pregnancy tests, and the empty bed she comes home to each night. But lying there each night in that bed, her hand rests over the tiny, secret cluster as she falls asleep. Every second that it stays there, under her hand, the cells are dividing into something bigger, something less easy to hide, something that she must eventually think about. It is terrifying. And yet she tries to imagine falling asleep now without it there, and she knows she could not.

So she books herself in, and attends her check-up. Everything is perfectly normal. Only for her, it is not.

Soon then, there will be a child in her flat. A child that will need clothes and toys and a place to sleep. She has none of those things for it. There must be lists you can find on the internet for this, from people who know better, who have thought this through. Lists and suggestions and helpful advice about sleeping and feeding and changing nappies. She stops still for a second in the middle of the crowds that clutter the pedestrian precinct. Nappies. She will need these too. Around her, people cluster and chatter and shout. A generator in the doughnut kiosk stutters into life.

This is how she finds herself in the baby section of the department store, in aisles of fussy doll-like dresses and dungarees and cardigans, picked out in pink and blue and white, or printed with animals and leaves. She wanders, dizzy, up and down the rows, picking up soft, cheerful items and then discarding them again. Does a baby really need all these trimmings? Net skirts for a baby girl who can't yet twirl in them, shoes for a boy who can't yet run? There is too much choice here, and yet, when it comes down to it, she doesn't have one. The decision has already been made for her, by one thoughtless afternoon with him and a tenacious, jealous bundle of their cells, which have entwined inside her and refused to let go.

You have time, she tells herself, for all this. There is still some time, at least. You can leave, and come back again tomorrow, or next month, or even the one after that. These things will all still be here then. She starts to walk back through the waves of tiny shirts, the miniature smocked lace skirts, the little, empty legs and arms of the babygros flopping from their hangers, and stops in front of a jewel-green sleepsuit. It is made from some sort of fluffy, brushed material that gives the colour a look of soft, frosted seaglass. She takes it to the counter.

On her way out, she walks through the soaps and bottles and perfume, right past the place where she had stood, clutching a jar of handcream, so many months ago. She allows herself to breathe in the heady, floral brightness of it for a second, and then she walks on.

At three months you can begin telling people. This is what the first leaflet says. It assumes your partner, your parents perhaps, will already know. The fresh-faced woman in the photo that accompanies this article, with one coy mani-cured hand over her cashmere-covered belly, has definitely told her husband already, and probably has a cosy, smiling mother waiting in the wings, proffering blankets and bottles and a wealth of experience. She closes the woman back under the folds of her cover and does not open any more of the leaflets.

She takes the green sleepsuit out of its plastic bag, and lays it on the table in front of her on top of the pile, smooth-ing out its creases and tucks to show the shape of the child that might one day fit in it. It had seemed so unbelievably small out there in the shop, but now, here on her kitchen table, it is almost impossibly large.

It is then that the doorbell rings. She scrambles up, away from her table and the spread of the sleepsuit, and goes to answer it.

The woman on the doorstep is tall, with broad shoulders and pale, milky skin splashed with freckles. Her hair is coppery red, and pulled back in a high, rough bun. Her face is familiar, and yet she knows she does not know her. She stands still, holding the edge of the front door, and tries to work it out.

Are you here for Lilian? she asks. I'm upstairs. She's the ground-floor flat.

No, the strange and yet not-strange woman says, I'm here to see you. She folds her arms, and adds, in a trembling attempt at sarcasm, well, if you'll actually let me past the door, of course.

It is those arms, that half-bold attitude, that makes the pieces of this person fall into place.

Harriet, she says.

I got your address off Dad's phone. I wondered how long you'd take to recognise me. Can I come in?

She hesitates, still with her hands on the door.

Harriet gives a small line of a smile. Five minutes, that's all, I promise. Don't worry, I'm not here to beat you up.

Now that she knows this woman to be Harriet, it is easier to recognise her in this older, taller version. The hair has darkened a little, and the teenage plumpness has been replaced with a solid, adult hardness of capable limbs and freckled skin drawn tighter over the bones in her face, revealing the pointed shape of Anna's jaw. She is not as delicately pretty as Anna, there is something of Marcus's height and force there too, but it gives her a presence that Anna always, somehow, seemed to lack.

She takes her straight through into the living room, and Harriet stands there, looking around. The room suddenly seems much smaller, shabbier. She tries to find her voice again.

I know you said you were only going to stay five minutes, she says, but do you want some tea, or a drink, all the same?

I'll take vodka, if you've got it, Harriet says, and then laughs abruptly. No, thank you, I'm fine.

They hover awkwardly, facing each other.

Look, she says, not sure what exactly the next sentence should be, but Harriet raises her hand to stop her.

I think, Harriet says, it is fairly obvious why I am here. That I know about you and Dad, I mean. Let's just get that out of the way now.

Did he tell you? she says.

Not that it's anything to do with you, but he told Mum, actually. And then obviously, he had to tell me pretty damn quickly. Before Mum had a chance to do it for him.

I'm sorry, she starts to say, but Harriet's hand is up again.

I also know he said you ended it. And that as far as you are concerned, it's over.

Yes, she says slowly. Her hand rises, unconsciously, to her stomach. That's true enough. It was never meant to happen, and it shouldn't have. It is – was – a mistake.

Well, Harriet says, yes, Clare, I think we all know *that*. Then she sighs and bites her lip. It flushes white and then floods red again. I'm sorry. I didn't actually come here just to be nasty, much as you may think that.

So why *are* you here? she says. She wants Harriet's looming presence to leave her room, her flat, her life as quickly as possible.

Harriet sighs again. The words tumble out, in the same teenage rush. So I know Mum isn't the easiest person to live with. God, out of everyone, I should know that. And that doesn't excuse what he did. But she needs Dad, she really does. And now it's all out in the open, I want them to have a chance to work it out. So it can all be like it was. Like before—

Before Tom.

He and Mum had an argument. I think it must have been the night the two of you ended whatever weird – thing – you were having. And apparently, that's when it all came out. And turns out one of the main reasons he gives for the whole idiocy is that he could talk to you about it all. And he couldn't talk to Mum.

We did talk a lot, she says. About Tom. About that holiday.

But you see, Mum won't talk about that. Not really. Not ever. It's been so many years since she mentioned it – him – I can't even count them.

She lets herself think about Harriet, a younger, angrier Harriet, stranded between these two silent parents, and a new loneliness where her brother should be.

But what about you? Can you talk to her? she says.

Harriet raises an eyebrow. I have tried – but he wasn't my bloody son, was he? Look, there's only two people in the world who know what it actually felt like, and it's them. That's it. That's all there's ever going to be. And now they deserve to be left in peace to try and get over it, together.

I can't imagine— she says, and then Harriet turns to face her, one hand on her hip.

Clare. I don't know why on earth you did it – or why you'd even want to do it – and really I'm not interested either. That's not why I'm here. I just want to know from you that it's over, really over. That you won't be getting in the way any more.

She breathes in and out, feeling that dark place in her

abdomen gently expand and subside with each rush of air. The last thing I want, she says truthfully, carefully, is to get in the way.

So I have your word, then? Harriet says, coming a little closer to her. That it's over?

As far as I'm concerned, she says, we ended it. It's over.

And you'll never contact him again?

She steps back, and folds her arms over her stomach. She takes another careful, deep breath. That's not something I can promise, Harriet. I'm sorry.

Harriet raises her hands in disbelief. Why the hell not? If it's over, why would you ever need to?

I don't know, she stammers. I don't want to get in the way. But I can't promise never to be in contact with him. What if one of us needed to be?

For fuck's sake, Harriet says. One simple thing, Clare. That's all I ask. After everything you've done, as well.

I'm sorry, she says, although with a flare of something bright and dark inside her, she realises she is not now, not really, not to this woman who has come into this place and demanded something she has no right to claim.

I think you should go now. The words tremble but they come out all the same, and she can hardly believe she dares to say them. She keeps holding her eyes on Harriet's narrow, green ones, and in the end it is Harriet who blinks and looks away.

This is unbelievable, Harriet spits, and she wants to say, I know. But she stays where she is and lets Harriet walk from the room first, tracking her one pace behind, to make sure she leaves.

But Harriet stops on her way past the kitchen door, and behind her, she comes to a halt too. As if she had always known it would happen like this, she watches the coppery head twist to look into the room, at the table that sits just inside the doorway.

Harriet's anger is not an anger that makes her stupid with its force, but strong and clear and sharp. She watches Harriet pick up the seaglass sleepsuit, and then see the leaflets beneath, and then look back at her with those furiously narrow, calculating eyes, up and down the whole darkly growing length of her. She does not – cannot – say anything.

For *fuck's* sake, Harriet says again. Her eyes are exactly the same colour as the sleepsuit in her hand.

*

1995

Everyone was quiet in the car, in a grey silence punctuated only by the occasional crackle of a cagoule. Clare was thinking hard about what Tom had told her. Jem could have meant something else, but Tom seemed so certain. There was definitely something about him, a slight wildness in his eye, that gave her an odd tingle of recognition. It could explain it.

'What's going on in that head of yours?' Josie said, and Clare managed a smile before turning her face away, looking at the hedges streaking past beside them. Tom was right, there was no point telling their parents. Even if they believed them, they could not do anything anyway.

They parked the car and walked up to the Little Chapel together, through a little lane flanked with more hedges. 'It's pretty, I tell you,' Anna said. 'Really, it is. Like a fairytale castle. It used to be Harriet's absolute favourite thing.'

'Yeah, like, years ago,' Harriet said.

And then they were coming up a small path towards a

bright, small building, with a low arched doorway picked out in hundreds of coloured pieces, and a tower above made of stones and shells and tiny, rich dots of blue.

'Oh, would you look at that,' Josie said. 'Isn't it lovely?'

They went in through the doorway. The grown-ups had to stoop, but it was a perfect size for Clare. It was as if this place had been built just for her. Inside too, all the walls and windows and the roof were encrusted with patterns made from the stones and shells and little pieces of tile of every colour. The sills of the windows had frosted green borders of seaglass, and in the corners of the room, steps wound up and away into other tiny, jewelled rooms.

It made her thrill with delight, even though she knew without even trying to look for it that there was no Place hiding in the Little Chapel. But maybe that didn't have to make it any less magic. 'It is lovely,' she agreed. 'I really like it.'

'It looks really pretty from far away, but it's all actually just broken plates,' Harriet said, standing quite close to the wall and running her fingers over the cracks of each piece. 'Isn't it, though? All just a lot of broken plates.'

After dinner that night, Marcus produced a small, mottled box with dented edges. 'What on earth is that?' Harriet said.

'Playing cards,' Marcus said. He clicked open the lid and slid out a sheaf of waxy black and red pictures. 'I found them in that drawer. Fancy a round of something?'

Beside Clare, Josie grinned. 'Oh god, how wonderful. I can't remember the last time I had a good game of cards.'

Marcus pushed the cards together into a neat-edged pile. 'What'll it be then, folks. Whist? Rummy? Twenty-one?'

Anna leant back in her chair and sighed. She took another

sip of wine. 'Whatever we play, you'll have to explain the rules to us, Marc,' she said. 'None of us know them, apart from you.'

'*I* know,' Josie said. There was an unfamiliar, sharp-edged spark in her voice that made Clare look at her. She was resting her elbows on the table, with her arms stretched out towards the cards. 'How about Rummy?' she suggested. 'It's easy enough to get on a first go.'

Marcus nodded. 'Sounds good to me.' He started to deal the cards out, and Josie, shining with eagerness, began to tell them the rules.

After one round, Tom got down from the table.

'I don't want to play any more,' he said. 'I'm going to bed.'

'Buddy,' Marcus said, 'we can play something else if you like.'

'I don't want to play,' Tom repeated. He rubbed his eyes with his hands. They looked rough and pink at the edges.

'Are you sick, Tom, darling?' Anna said. She got up too, and put a hand to his forehead. 'You're cold. But then you're always a bit cold. I don't think he's running a temperature, Marc, but even so.'

'I'm just tired,' Tom said. 'That's all.'

Anna stood over him, hands on hips. 'Maybe you do just need a good sleep,' she said.

'I'm sure that's all it is,' Marcus said. 'Go on to bed, Tom.'

'I'll be in to check on you later,' Anna said.

Tom stopped on his way to the door. 'I don't want you to do that. I told you I was fine.'

'Okay, then,' Marcus said easily, collecting up cards and tapping them into a stack on the table. 'Whatever you want.'

Tom left the room. Anna sat back down again and sighed. 'Honestly, I just don't know—' Her eyes met Clare's and she stopped, abruptly. 'Well, then.'

'It's way more fun without him being all moody and drippy anyway,' Harriet said.

'No more of that, thank you very much,' Marcus said, in his heavy voice that showed he meant it. 'Now, Clare, shall we have another game?'

'I don't mind,' Clare said, 'if we play this one again.'

'Fine by me,' Josie said. There was that glint again in her voice. Marcus passed her the cards and her thin fingers, suddenly and surprisingly powerful, rippled over them, sliding and slicing them together so fast that Clare couldn't see where one card ended and another began. She could have watched her mother do this forever, but she knew that the cards had to be dealt, in the end.

'But it's not *fair*. Josie didn't shuffle the cards properly.'

'Sometimes you get lucky and sometimes you don't, Harriet,' Marcus said. 'That's how it goes.'

'You're only saying that because you did really well,' Harriet spat.

'For heaven's sake, Harriet,' Anna said, resting her forehead against her palm, 'it's only a *game*.'

'You ready for bed, bug?' Josie said, in Clare's ear. 'Let's go up, eh?'

Upstairs in their room, with the door closed, Josie gave a sigh and flopped down on her bed. 'My god, and to think Harriet isn't even a proper teenager yet.'

'Is that what happens, then?' Clare said. 'When you become a teenager?' She thought of all Harriet's strange, sharp edges.

Josie stared up at the ceiling, her face framed in the

billow of the duvet. 'Sometimes,' she said. 'Sometimes not. It's hard to tell.'

Josie was obviously in a talkative mood. She wasn't often, with Clare. It felt like a very grown-up conversation to be having, and inside, Clare was giddy and shaky with the happening of it. If she could only ask the right questions, she could make it last for just a little while longer.

'What were you like?' she tried, shyly. 'As a teenager?'

'Me? Oh god,' Josie laughed up at the woven wicker of the lampshade. 'I was horrible.'

'Like Harriet?'

'*Worse* than Harriet. So much worse.'

'Really?' Clare tried to imagine this and had to give up.

Josie sat up. 'Appalling. I used to run away from home, and all sorts. But don't you go getting any ideas now. You're not allowed to become a teenager.'

'I'm not?' Clare said.

Josie shook her head, half a smile crawling into the corner of her mouth. 'No way. Not ever. I want you to stay just exactly as you are.'

'But I don't think I want to change, anyway,' Clare said. 'I want to carry on being exactly the same.'

Josie's smile faltered and slipped off the side of her lips. She was suddenly older, more tired. 'Sometimes, you don't get a choice, little bug. Sometimes, changes just happen without you being able to do anything about them.'

She came and sat next to Clare, on her bed. 'Although they can be for the best, in the end.' She put a hand on Clare's head, and smoothed her hair, down, and down, and down again. With her other hand, she picked up the Treasure Stone from the bedside table, and looked at it against the lamplight. 'But who knows,' she said, more quietly, 'maybe you'll be able to stay just the same in the important ways, just like you want.'

Clare leaned towards her, into the dip of her weight on the bed, and Josie rested her hand, for one more moment, on Clare's head. Then she dropped her hand again, and Clare knew the conversation was over.

When Clare woke up, it was dark, and she could hear footsteps on the landing, going back and forth, and loud voices. She lay there, listening, waiting for the thuds to subside back into quietness again, but they did not. Then Josie started to turn in her own bed, with purposeful rustles that meant that she was awake too.

'Mum,' Clare said into the darkness, 'what is it?'

There was another rustle, and then a click, and Josie's face, yellow and creased, was leaning towards her, her hand on the lamp switch. Clare blinked.

'I don't know,' Josie said. 'It sounds like Marcus and Anna are up. I ought to go and see, I suppose.' She lifted her watch up to her face. 'Two forty-five. Christ almighty.' She rolled her feet down to the ground and reached for the dressing gown on the end of the bed. 'You stay here.'

Clare waited until Josie had left the room, drawing the door closed with a hard click behind her, before getting up and tiptoeing towards it. She opened the door again a crack, and sat down on the floor beside it, listening. Voices bounced up the walls from the hallway, the echo making them sound important, serious, like a film on the television.

'And we've checked everywhere in the house, we're certain?' Marcus.

'I can't think of anywhere we haven't,' Anna, muffled.

'Did you look in the garden yet?' This was Josie now, clearer, calmer than the other two. 'I can go look in the garden.'

'Oh, for god's sake, Harriet, why didn't you say something sooner?' Anna again, higher.

'I didn't know, okay?' Harriet now. 'I thought he was just sulking somewhere. I didn't know he was properly *gone*. Not until I woke up just now.'

'Anna,' Marcus said, 'come on, darling, this isn't helping.'

'My son is missing,' Anna said. '*Missing*, Marcus. Don't you dare—'

'Let's check the garden quickly, right now,' Marcus said. 'And then, if he's not there, I'm ringing the police.'

'Oh god,' Anna said. 'Oh god.'

From the window of the bedroom, Clare watched the beams of two torches, criss-crossing over the grass, flickering in the branches of the trees. A dark figure paced round the shed, shining a light into the windows and over the door, while another traced a circle around the shadowy stone of the walls. Maybe he had gone up into the trees, she thought. Or managed to find a way into that shed. He wouldn't have gone back *there* again, would he? Not without her. She gripped the windowsill, hoping for a shout, another smaller figure slipping out of the darkness and into the torch beam.

But the lights were coming back towards her now, the long triangles of light from the torches growing shorter until they disappeared below her. He was not there. There was only one other place he might be, and it was only her who knew it. She took a deep breath, left the window, and ran towards the door.

When they saw her upstairs, looking down from the landing into the hallway, they all stopped talking, and looked up towards her, their faces oddly round. Harriet and Anna's eyes were puffy, the skin around them mottled with red. Josie was wearing a dressing gown and a pair of muddy green wellingtons that made her feet giant, clown-like. And Marcus stood paused, by the dresser, twisting the wire of the telephone in his fingers.

'Bug,' Josie said, too gently, shuffling forward in the wellingtons to the foot of the stairs. 'Come down here.'

Clare ran down the stairs, and Josie took her into her arms. The fabric of the dressing gown was cold and smelt of fresh earth. 'Tom's missing,' she said.

'That's right,' Josie said, just as gently. 'Now look, you won't be in trouble or anything, but if you know where Tom might be, we need to know. Do you think there's anywhere he might have gone on his own?'

'Any place. Any at all. Even if there's only a little chance, Clare,' Marcus said. 'All the same, we need to know.'

'I know,' Clare said. She lifted her face from Josie's sleeve and looked up into Marcus's dark, tired eyes. They had to know. There was nothing else she could do. 'He said he wanted to go back to the beach, you know, the one with the caves.'

'Oh, no,' Marcus said.

'What caves?' Anna said. 'Marcus, tell me, what caves?'

'The ones we saw the other morning, yes?' Marcus said, coming closer.

Clare nodded. 'When the tide was out. He said he wanted to go back down when the tide was out.'

Anna gave a strange sob that was almost a wail, and sunk down on to the bottom step of the stairs. 'Mum?' Harriet said.

Marcus was already punching numbers into the phone, listening to it ring out. 'I'm calling them and then I'm going down there. Straight away.'

Clare could not look at Marcus any more, at the desperate way he clutched the phone, so she turned her head back towards the stairs. Harriet stood over her mother, tear-stained, stock still, horrified.

The police arrived, some time after that, and then everything seemed to go very fast and yet incredibly slowly, all at once. Marcus came and went and came again, and a man in a uniform sat at the dining table, making notes and talking to Anna. Josie took Harriet and Clare into the living room, and brought their duvets down from their beds. 'You can watch the television, if you like,' she told them, but there was nothing on except Open University programmes about the solar system and chemistry. Harriet bunched down in her duvet and refused to talk, which was just as well, as Clare couldn't think of anything to say.

After a while, Josie came in, and in her new gentle voice she told Clare that the policeman wanted to speak to her about what she'd told Marcus, and would she mind talking to them? She didn't have to, if she didn't want to, but it might help them find Tom sooner, if she could. And Josie would be there with her too, of course.

Clare was not used to this soft, trembling Josie. It made her feel scared and worried about Tom in a way she hadn't been before. She let Josie lead her through into the kitchen, and sat down beside her, opposite the policeman.

The policeman was balding, with deep, bruised bags under his eyes. He wrote slowly on a pad in front of him, and the fingers that held the pen had surprising amounts of dark hair just below the knuckles. Clare stared at them, until she realised he might think she was staring at what he was writing, so she tried to look down at the table in front of her instead.

The policeman asked her about the morning walk with Marcus and Tom, the beach, the caves, in dizzying detail. 'And tell me, do you have any idea why he might have wanted to go back there?' he said.

Clare hesitated. 'He liked caves,' she said. 'He – we liked places you could get into and disappear. Like … caves and things. We tried to find them.'

The policeman nodded. 'Ah, it was a sort of game, a bit of fun, for you two, yes?'

She struggled to find words. 'Sort of,' she said. 'But not – like this. Never like this.' She shivered, and Josie put her arm around her.

The policeman smiled. 'I was the same, as a kid,' he said. 'Now look, Clare. We're doing our very best to find him. We've got a search team and a coastguard patrol out there, and they'll be looking all along the stretch of cliff you've told us about. If he's down there, we can't miss him.'

He flipped the page of his notebook over. 'Thank you for everything you've said. You've been a great help. Before you go, is there anything else you'd like to tell me that you think might be important? Any little thing that you think I might have missed?'

A crack, a shadow, Tom turning to look back at her as he slipped through. There were no words for this, no way to make this real, if it was real at all. 'No,' she said. 'No, thank you.'

Josie took her out then, and bundled her back up in her duvet, upstairs in bed. 'Sleep,' she said. 'Or try to, at any rate. You need it. You did well tonight, with the policeman. It was a great help. I'm proud of you.'

'Will you come up soon?' Clare said.

'I'd better stay up, for now,' Josie said. 'I think the others might need me. You don't mind, do you?'

'No,' Clare said, although she wanted Josie to stay right there, in bed beside her, like it was the beginning of the night and they were still asleep and none of this had happened.

'There'll be more news in the morning, I expect,' Josie said. 'They'll have come back from their search. Maybe, by the time you wake up, he'll even be back here with us.'

'I hope so,' Clare said.

'Me too.' Josie kissed her on the forehead, more firmly than usual, and then switched off the light.

Yes, there were caves down there below the high tide waterline, the coastguard men said. They'd taken a boat out straight away, into the cove, with their searchlights, as close as they could to the rocks. But it was high tide when they got there, and the caves were all filled up with water. There wasn't a chance, they said, that anyone could survive in them. Not like that, when the water's up. There would be nowhere inside for anyone to go.

11

Farewell to the Island

For the next few days, she waits for the world to end.

This could happen in a number of ways, of course. An asteroid could strike Earth, causing the sea to swell up and come crashing down over the tight rows of terraces, the cold water smashing into her flat and carrying her body back out again with it. A terrible, mutated virus could come to the town, and she could watch from the window as quietly, slowly, the traffic stopped moving down the road and she dwindled into a pale shadow behind the curtains. There could be fires, bombs, alien invasions. Or he could get in touch with her to say yes, he knows, and what are they going to do about it.

It is on Friday that it finally happens. No seas, no fires, just one dreadful, bright flash of her phone on the table.

I know you said you didn't want me to contact you, he says, in a formal little speech bubble on her phone's screen. But it seems there is a reason we should talk soon. Please can we meet tomorrow?

A pause, and then another bubble blossoms. I want you to know, I will fully support you in whatever you choose to do. I won't be difficult. I won't make anything any harder than it is. I just think we should talk about it.

She knows she must reply, but she dreads having to type the words to do it. She leaves it as long as possible before texting back and having to accept that tomorrow, at eleven, is when it will be over.

When she arrives at the cafe, he is already there, sitting at a table towards the front of the shop that is partly shielded from the rest of the tables by an uneven corner and a bookcase. She notes the thoughtfulness that has gone into this choice, that will have gone into this meeting. He gets up, a little awkwardly, shuffling out from between the chair legs to face her, and then stops, uncertain whether to kiss, to hug.

She gives him a smile and then sits down, unkissed. He folds himself back down into his own chair.

I haven't ordered yet, he says.

I think you have to go to the counter, she says.

Well, I'll go, then, he says. She knows from the tremble in his voice that he is trying to sound light and relaxed. What will you have?

A cappuccino, please, she says, and then pauses. Actually, I suppose it should be decaf.

He shakes his head, looks down at the table, and sighs. Well, yes, he says, I suppose it should.

While he is at the counter, shuffling along the glass front in a line of people, she watches him. He seems just like any other man in that queue, checking the menu board, making his order, feeling in a pocket for his wallet. He is unremarkable, casual, in a jacket and trousers that could belong to anybody, a head of grey hair that could be found on any other man of his age. She cannot quite believe that once she ran her fingers over this middle-aged man's shoulder, slid a hand over his bare leg, counted each freckle on his back. It seems a fantastical bewitching, a story she would have told herself and never believed could be true. She marvels.

We have both been bewitched, she thinks, and now we are awake.

He comes towards her, and sets down two white, solid cups.

So then, he says.

I would have told you myself, you know, she says. Eventually, I would have told you.

Harriet shouldn't have come over like that, he says. But all the same, I'm glad that I know.

She feels her voice rising. I didn't know myself, until very recently. But I had a scan. And everything's fine.

So then, he repeats. He plays with the rim of his cup. Forgive me for being indelicate, but I take it that means you are planning to have – it?

It's been three months, she says, I sort of have to, now. But yes, I was. I am, I mean.

I see, he says.

When it came down to it, I couldn't do anything else.

He puts his hand to his forehead. I didn't mean – I mean, I wasn't asking you to do anything else.

I know, she assures him. Really, I do know that.

I can't really believe this is happening, he says. Not yet.

He picks up his cup and she watches the brown surface of the coffee ripple as he tries to steady his fingers. She remembers reading somewhere, not so long ago, about how the body's ability to cope with shock diminishes with age.

Take it slowly, she says. We've got some time.

He swallows and sets the cup carefully down. You know, I really didn't see it at the time, he says, measuring out the words, but it was all wrong. For both of us, it was all wrong.

I think we were just sort of – I don't know – using the other one to prop ourselves up, if that makes sense? And so that, that was fine. But now this. *This*. What do we do about this? I mean, what do you want? If anything?

She cradles her own cup in her hands. I don't know, she says. I don't know how to go about this bit at all.

It's not something I ever thought of, he says, to the ceiling above him. Having a child. Like this.

The table between them seems so wide, the chair he sits in so far away.

It was that last time it happened, she says. At mine.

That last time, he says, and she sees the grey of the storm clouds scud across his face, in his eyes the heat rising from the radiators. Yes, of course it was. That very last time.

They talk in this way for a while, going back and forth with polite, thoughtful expressions of disbelief and surprise, until the cups are empty, and they have to find a decision in the bottom of them.

Clare, look, he says, I want to be involved. I won't push myself on you, but I would like to know the baby.

I don't know how it's going to work, she says. I haven't really thought about it yet. She tries to imagine him turning up at her house one afternoon to change nappies, make tea, sit in her living room rocking a sleeping child. The image starts to make her breathless, uneasy.

Well, look, just count me in, all right? he says. When you do think about it. Please. Just keep in touch.

He is trying to be patient, he is trying to be kind. She recognises this. I will, she says. I promise, I will.

Thank you, he says.

I know it's your child too, she says, as they say goodbye outside the cafe, with a careful hug from which she tries not to flinch away. I won't forget that. They'll always be your daughter or son too.

My daughter, he says, wondering. My son.

As soon as she gets through the front door, she kicks off her sandals and starts to undress, pulling off her cardigan, wresting her dress up over her head and losing herself, for a moment, in a circle of fabric before shaking it off into a pile in the hallway. Her bra is tight – has been too tight for a little while now – and the wires are damp and hot against her ribs. She unhooks it, and slides her arms free, letting it fall to the carpet.

The bedroom curtains are closed against the sun. She goes to the mirror and looks at her bare skin in the half dark, at the body which is hers and yet not hers, the body which has taken something that belonged to someone else. And it is something she cannot ever return, a loan that can never be repaid. She will be accountable for what she has taken, to him, to his child, forever. There will be no more quiet patches of darkness, no more Places just out of reach. She will never be wholly alone and whole again.

I can't do it, she says, into the hot, dusty darkness. I just can't.

There is only one thing left that she can still think to do. She dresses again, leaves the house and starts to walk towards the station.

She waits until the taxi driver has pulled away into the darkness, and she is alone on the street. Then she walks up to the door and presses the doorbell, firmly, twice, so it cannot be mistaken.

After a pause, the door opens. The woman who answers it is wrapped in an old, bobbled dressing gown, one hand still adjusting the sash over her hip. The hallway is dark behind her, with light scattering down the staircase from above. She shakes her head. You idiot, bug, she says. You stupid, bloody idiot.

And then Josie's arms spring open and snap her closed into a surprising hug, and they do not let go again.

*

1995

'Bug, you don't have to come out on the search party. You can stay here. I'll get Alexa to come over.'

'I want to,' Clare said. 'Please let me.'

Josie bent down so that she was face to face with Clare. She had deep grey circles swimming around both of her eyes. 'There'll be lots of other people there. You don't have to come. It's perhaps better if you stay here, rest.'

'I want to go,' Clare said again. If only she could get down there, see for herself, then maybe she could find him.

Josie considered. 'Well, all right then. But you have to promise to stick next to me, and if I think you look tired, we're coming straight home, all right?'

As soon as the coastguard left, Marcus had gone back out with the policemen to continue searching for Tom. Anna and Harriet went out to join them a little while later, and then it was just Josie and Clare, alone together in the silent kitchen. Josie made some toast, but neither of them felt hungry, so the toast just sat there between them with a greasy slick of butter, gradually curling upwards on the plate.

The policeman had been all along the local roads, Josie told her, knocking on doors and asking people if they'd seen anything, asking them to check their houses and to help with the search down on the cliffs, if they could.

'But Tom wouldn't have gone into somebody else's house, would he?' Clare said.

Josie shrugged and grimaced. 'They're doing what they can, bug. They have to make sure they've gone through all the possibilities.'

'What possibilities are there, though?'

Josie stood up, and started to gather their plates together, scraping the pieces of toast into a pile. 'You should stay here,' she said. 'Really, you should.'

'You already said I could go,' Clare reminded her.

Josie dumped the plates into the sink, suddenly sharp. 'Fine. Fine! But when I say we're coming back, we're coming back, all right? No arguments. No scenes.'

'I wouldn't do that.' Clare was aggrieved. 'You know I wouldn't.'

She watched Josie's back at the sink slope into a sigh. 'I'm sorry, bug,' she said, turning round. 'I know that.' She wiped her hands and came back over to the table, putting her hand on Clare's shoulder. 'This is a really upsetting situation, for all of us. I'm just trying to protect you.'

'I don't need protecting,' Clare said. 'I just want to help.'

Josie squeezed her shoulder. 'I don't know what I'd do,' she said, very quietly, 'if I lost you.'

They were searching a section of the cliff and the beaches near the footpath entrance that they thought Tom might have used. It was hard to believe it had only been two days ago that they had run through that gate on their way to the beach. Now there were policemen there standing in the road, in official-looking jackets, holding radios, and two big, stern dogs in harnesses. Clare could see heads and shoulders sprouting from the gorse at intervals along the cliff path, twisting, stooping, talking.

She closed her eyes for a moment to see if she could still feel the tingle drawing her down towards the cliff, but there was nothing there at all. Everything here seemed flatter today, less colourful, as if somebody had bleached and ironed the grass and sea and rocks and folded them up in front of her into a tidy pile. It was as if there never was a Place there at all. Could she – they – just have imagined it? Imagined all of them? She thought about the policeman's words – 'a sort of game, a bit of fun' – and shivered at the solidity of them.

'We should find Marcus and Anna,' Josie said. She asked one of the policemen which way they had gone, and he directed them down the cliff path that led to the viewpoint, the same one from where Clare and Tom and Marcus had first seen the second cove.

They followed the path down, passing an older couple, in matching cagoules, pushing their way tentatively into a cluster of bushes. 'There's a lot of people here who aren't police,' Josie said. 'That's good.'

'Why is that good?'

'Well, lots of people have turned up to help look. The more people who are looking, the more chance they have of finding him.'

Clare felt cold, even though it wasn't particularly cold or windy, not today. 'Mum,' she said, stopping on the path. 'They will find him, won't they? I mean, they have to.' He had to be somewhere. And even if it was true, even if Tom had managed to find one, he would have to come out, eventually.

Josie paused, and bit her lip. Clare could tell, before she even started to speak, that she was not going to say what Clare was hoping to hear. 'Oh, bug,' Josie said. 'I don't know. But we all hope so.'

When they came out on to the cliff edge, it was to see Marcus and Anna standing there with Harriet, looking out over the bay.

'I just don't understand,' Anna was saying, 'I just don't understand what would make him go down there. In the night, Marcus. On his own.'

'How do we even know he went down there?' Harriet asked.

'Well, all we know for sure is he made it as far as the cliff path,' Marcus said.

Anna pushed her hair back from her face. 'But Clare seemed to think—'

She broke off, and looked up as she saw Clare and Josie picking their way down the path towards them.

Josie took hold of Clare's hand, even though she was too big for that now, really. 'We came to help with the search,' Josie said. 'Has there been any more news?'

'A neighbour from this end of the road saw him walking down the road towards the cliff, about eleven o'clock last night,' Marcus said. 'He was on his own, just walked past her front gate.'

'A little boy, all on his own,' Anna said. 'And she didn't think—' Her voice rose and cracked, abruptly, halfway through the sentence.

'Mum,' Harriet said, but less forcefully than she usually might have done.

Marcus shrugged. 'She said she thought he was one of the kids from the holiday let next door. I suppose there must be so many.'

'Even so,' Anna said. She crossed her arms and turned away from them all, looking out over the waves.

'This is the place, isn't it?' Harriet said to Clare. 'The place you thought he wanted to go?'

Clare held Josie's hand tighter. 'Yes,' she said. 'This is the place we saw when we came down.' She looked up at Marcus for reassurance and he nodded.

'Can we get down?' Clare asked Josie. 'To the caves, I mean.'

'The tide's up again,' Harriet said. 'Mum wanted to … to see what you were talking about, but we can't. But she doesn't want to wait.'

'For fuck's sake, Harriet!' Anna spat the words over the cliff top.

'Anna!' That was Marcus.

Clare looked quickly away and down. Far below in the water, two red and white boats bobbed up near the rocks. On one, a tiny, bright wetsuited figure was climbing over the side and down into the darkness beneath.

After that, Josie said, 'I think I'm taking Clare back to the house,' and Clare did not even try to protest.

She looked over at Marcus, and he nodded. 'Harriet, you want to come?' Josie asked.

'I'm fine here,' Harriet said. Anna did not turn around.

'Why don't you go with Josie?' Marcus said, walking back over to his daughter.

'I'm fine here,' Harriet repeated, looking at the ground.

'Go on, Harri,' Marcus said, putting his arm over her shoulders. 'Go back on up with Josie.'

It wasn't a question. Harriet shrugged her body out from under his arm and stood back. 'Fine,' she said. 'Whatever.' She pushed her hands further into the front pocket of her sweatshirt and started to stalk back up along the path.

Josie gave Marcus a small, tentative smile. 'Don't worry about her. We'll look after her.'

'Thank you,' Marcus said. He managed a smile back,

a grey, falling-off sort of a smile that didn't quite make it up into his cheeks, and then it collapsed away again. Josie reached out to touch his arm, just for a second, and then she squeezed Clare's hand, still clasped in hers. 'Come on. Let's catch up with Harriet.'

They walked quickly away, up the path. As they reached the turn, Clare twisted her head back towards the viewing point. Anna had not moved, and Marcus was standing where they had left him, looking up into the gorse with that blank, terrible face.

Harriet was still several paces in front of them as they got to the gate that led back to the road. The policemen standing there stopped her, so Clare and Josie caught up with her. 'See,' Harriet was saying, 'they're right here.'

'It's all right,' Josie said, 'we're together. We're going back to the house, if that's all right.'

The man nodded. 'No problem.'

'Come on,' Harriet said. She was already through the gate. They all walked side by side up the road, Josie in the middle.

'Hey,' a voice said, to the left of them, with a gruff seriousness to it. 'Hello.'

They turned together, to see Jem coming out of one of the houses on the left side of the road, wearing his battered coat, his hair pulled back into the same ponytail. Clare moved a little further behind Josie. So this was where he lived.

'Oh, hello,' Josie said. 'Hello, Jem.'

'I won't keep you,' Jem said, coming to meet them in the middle of the road. 'I just wanted to say how sorry I am to hear about your boy. About Tom.'

'Oh,' Josie said, 'oh, well, he's not – but – well, that's kind of you to say. Thank you.'

Jem sighed and blew out his reddened cheeks. 'I told the police already, but I saw him yesterday morning down on those cliffs. Messing about, right up close to the edge. I told him off and sent him home. But I wish I'd done more now.'

Clare thought again about what Tom had told her, out in the garden. Was that all it had been then? She looked up at Jem, an older man, wheezing slightly, squinting into the sunshine, and could not feel the shiver any more. Had it ever, really, been there?

'Oh, no, no, I'm sure you did what you could,' Josie said. 'At the time.'

'I'm just going down now,' Jem said. 'To help search.'

'That's kind,' Josie said. 'Thank you. I'll tell Tom's parents.'

'Oh, I'm sorry,' Jem said. 'I thought you were his mum?'

Harriet laughed, and Josie took a step back abruptly. 'No,' she said, her voice high, 'oh no. That's Anna. I'm … Clare's mine. But Harriet here and Tom, they're Anna and Marcus's.'

Jem nodded. 'My mistake, I'm sorry. Ah, I hope he's found, and soon. There's lots of caves down there, you know – I used to go in all the time as a boy, myself. Plenty of places he could be hiding in.'

He winked at Clare, and to her surprise, she found herself smiling back, even though it felt disloyal to Tom, somehow.

The house was full of people that afternoon, coming and going. Marcus and Anna had taken over the kitchen, and police officers arrived, and then left again, only to be replaced by others. The front door kept opening and shutting, and Clare sat in her room and tried to read, but the words kept blurring and butting each other off the edge of the pages.

If Tom had got in, she thought, how long would it be possible for him to stay there? It was hard to tell, but when she had been inside, it felt like it could only be seconds, maybe minutes. And yet she was convinced she had slid books into those tiny ones at home that she'd kept there for months, without any difficulty. That was, if the books had actually been in there at all. If the Places were really there at all.

Even so, he could have taken her with him when he went to find them, just like he promised he would. She snapped her book shut and pushed it to the end of the bed with one foot.

After a while, there were no more footsteps in the hallway, and the door stopped slamming. There was a knock on Clare's door, and Josie popped her head around the edge. 'All right in here?' she said.

'Did they find anything?' Clare said, even though she knew the answer already from the sad, tired look on Josie's face. 'Anything at all?'

Josie came inside the room and shut the door. 'No,' she said, very softly, 'I'm afraid they didn't.' She sat down on Clare's bed. 'They're all gone for today. Do you want to come down and have something to eat?'

Downstairs, Anna and Marcus were still sitting in the kitchen, Harriet leaning on the sideboard behind them. The chairs were all pulled out at awkward angles around the table, a stack of mugs clustered together at its centre.

'Did they have to go through my things too?' Harriet said.

Marcus rubbed his eyes. 'I don't think so, Harri,' he said. 'They just needed to search Tom's belongings. Just to be sure there wasn't anything there.'

'I think they went through my things too,' Harriet said, darkly. 'They're all in the wrong places.'

'Does it matter?' Marcus said. 'I'm sure they won't have harmed them.'

'Shall I make some pasta?' Josie said. 'For the kids, at least. I think we should all try and eat something.'

'Not for me,' Anna said, staring at the table.

'Marcus?'

He looked up at her. 'It might be an idea.'

'I don't know how you can eat,' Anna said. 'At a time like this.' She was whiter than Clare had ever seen her, her skin pulled taut across her cheekbones.

'We all have to eat, love,' Marcus said. 'We have to keep on doing that, at least.' He reached across the table, and put his hand on top of hers, but she pulled it back, out of his reach.

'I can't,' Anna said. 'I can't.' Her voice cracked again, just as it had on the cliff top. She pushed back her chair and stood up. 'Enjoy your lovely family meal,' she said, trembling. '*I* am going to go upstairs and think about our son.'

She left the room. In the silence, Clare did not quite know where to look, so she stared down at her feet instead, and flexed her toes in her socks.

'I'm sorry, Jos,' Marcus said.

'For heaven's sake,' Josie said, her voice low, 'there's nothing to be sorry for. I'll cook the kids some tea.'

'Dad,' Harriet said. 'Aren't you going to see if Mum's okay?'

Marcus got up from the table, and put his arms around Harriet. 'I will,' he said. 'Let's just give her a moment, eh?'

Josie started to pull pans out of the cupboard and then paused, setting a pan down on the side. 'Look, Marcus,' she started, and then stopped again. 'Clare and I, we can go. I want to help, you know I do, and if you want us to stay, we can, but I can't help feeling we're in the way here.'

Marcus turned to face her, one hand still around Harriet's shoulder. 'Oh, Josie,' he said. 'You know you're not in the way. But you've got Clare to think of too.'

'We can stay if you want,' Josie said. 'We can. I just think—' She broke off, and picked up a pan lid. 'Well,' she finished, 'that it might be best, that's all.'

'Take Harriet,' Marcus said, suddenly.

Harriet sprang back out of his arms. 'No! I'm fine here.'

'Please,' Marcus said. 'Harri, this is no place for you to be. Not right now. Grandma's already offered to have you to stay. Wouldn't that be nicer than here?'

'You just want to be rid of me.' Harriet said. 'All the time, you just want to be rid of me.'

'That's not true at all,' Marcus said. 'You know that. But we need to find Tom right now. If it was you who had gone missing, we'd be doing the same.'

'I bet you wouldn't,' Harriet said, but her face had begun to droop with the same tired look as Marcus's.

Marcus pulled her to him again. 'Please don't fight me on this one, Harri,' he said. 'Not now. Please, go with Josie, and stay at Grandma's. Just for a bit, until we—' He stopped.

'I'll go and give the office a ring now,' Josie said, gently. 'With any luck, I'll catch them before they close.' She went through into the front hall.

'Come on now,' Marcus said to Harriet. He kept his arms tight around her, and Harriet let him, pressing her face into his shirt, snuffling slightly against the material. She was crying properly now, her shoulders heaving up and down. Clare felt as if she had made herself invisible, as if she had somehow slipped away into the cracks in the kitchen tiles, unnoticed. It was an uncomfortable spell to have woven. She stood and watched them, because she could do nothing else.

'It will all be all right again,' Marcus said, to the top of his daughter's tousled head. 'It will, I promise.'

Josie came back in, holding her purse and a piece of paper with a series of numbers scribbled down on it. She stood in the doorway, sliding the zip up and down on her purse.

'I've managed to get the three of us tickets on the midday flight,' she said. 'We can leave tomorrow morning.'

Harriet did not speak. All the way to the airport, she sat in silence in the back of the taxi, with her earphones glued into her ears. Clare looked out of the window, at the fields and fences rushing by. The sun had come out again. If they had still been on holiday, this would definitely have been a beach day.

The taxi driver was quiet too, and at the airport, while Josie was fishing in her bag for her purse, he disappeared for a moment and returned pushing a trolley. He loaded their suitcases on to it, stacking them carefully in order of size, while Josie waited, helplessly, with her purse in her hand.

'Honestly, we're fine,' she kept saying. 'Honestly. The girls and I will be fine from here.'

Finally, the man straightened up, and waved away the notes Josie held out to him. 'No, thank you, but no,' he said. 'This one's on me.'

'Oh no,' Josie said, 'please.'

The taxi driver shook his head. 'I hope they find him, ma'am. Really, I hope they do.'

Josie's face became blank and still. She blinked, once, twice, and her mouth opened. 'Thank you,' she managed, eventually.

The man got back in his car and drove off. Josie steadied her hands on the bar of the trolley, but did not start to push it.

'How did he know?' Clare said. 'Mum, how did he know?'

'That's island life for you,' came a voice from behind them. Harriet, her arms crossed, leaning against a concrete pillar. 'Everyone's stalking everyone, round here.'

'You don't want to eat?'

Clare stared down at the sandwich on her tray. They had let Harriet have the window seat on the plane, for reasons that Josie had not needed to explain. Harriet had been awful all day, cross with Josie and ignoring Clare whenever she tried to speak to her. Yet Josie had continued to use a special, nicer voice than normal, even though Clare could tell she was desperate to tell her off, just as she would have done with Clare.

'No,' Clare said. 'I'm not hungry.'

'Try a bit,' Josie said. 'Just a bit. There won't be anything else till we land and get home, you know. And you'll be hungry.'

Harriet was flicking the ashtray cover in her armrest, up and down, up and down. 'If she doesn't want her sandwich, bagsy it,' she said. 'I'm starving.'

Clare wondered how she would act, if she were Harriet. Wouldn't a sister cry, look sad, be upset? Harriet was just crosser than usual. Was this how it would be, to lose a brother? She realised she would never know.

Josie ignored Harriet. 'Just try and eat a bit for me, bug,'

The metal ashtray clicked and clicked.

It was strange to be back in the flat again, walking deep into the chilly, undisturbed smell of a place that had been closed up for over a week. Everything was exactly as Clare had left it in her room, but when she picked up pens and books and toys, they felt as if they belonged to someone else, not her at all. She looked at them, and they were suddenly entirely different things, from a different life.

Josie was unpacking in the main room, pulling clothes briskly out of suitcases and sorting them into washing piles on the floor. She didn't seem to want any help, so Clare went back into her room and sat down on the bed. She thought about Harriet, going off stiffly with her grandmother's arm around her, and Marcus and Anna, alone together in the cottage, and Tom, out there still, somewhere in the darkness. Why hadn't he taken her? And if she had only gone with him, maybe she could have persuaded him to return, helped him find his way back through, just like she'd promised. If he was even there, of course.

In a sudden rush of guilt and hope, she snapped the light off, picked up the small mirror that sat on the table beside her bed and stared hard into it. The light from the street lamp outside her window came through the half-open curtains, and threw glinting, orangey shapes on to the wall behind her. They bounced into the mirror and disappeared down into it as she twisted and craned.

'Tom?' she tried, in a whisper, and then more daring, aloud, 'Tom?'

All she could see was the gleam of her own eye in the dark.

12

The Last Voyage

In that last month, she knows you are meant to have a surge of energy. People tell tales of moving house, cleaning the attic, waters breaking halfway up a stepladder in the nursery, paint roller in hand. She finds none of this urgency. Her body seems content to be propped up by pillows on a sofa, to pace between bedroom and kitchen and bathroom, to amble down to the shop and back again.

Friends like Meena come over, friends without children, who hold their hands against her belly and laugh with amazement. They ask if she is scared of the birth. She does not know. She knows she is scared of not being at work, of being here, of the days and the months and the years – yes, years – stretching out in front of her.

He will not be with her at the birth. This has been decided.

I feel like I should, he says, on the phone. Be there, I mean.

Maybe it's easier if you don't, she says. Easier for both of us. My mother has already offered.

We should sort something out soon, he says, something, you know, about money. I want you to understand – you don't have to worry …

Afterwards, she says, afterwards.

I could come over, he said, any time, if you need anything.

Afterwards, she says.

And, if she is honest, she craves these last times alone. It is then that she can believe most clearly in a dark gap in the corner of the stair, an extra silver flicker in a mirror. It is a lot easier to imagine the son waiting on the other side of the divide without his father here, anchoring her to this one.

It is in those last close nights it all comes back more vividly to her. She cannot sleep. Even when she lies down, her body seems too heavy to bear. She thinks she might like to write something down. She wants to hold a pen, feel the words pressed out through her fingers in a firm black line.

She feels her child pushing against the swollen curve of her stomach, in unconscious sympathy. She finds her child's foot and tries to cup the heel in the palm of her hand. I am trying to recognise you, she tells her small, faceless child, I am trying to know you. I am trying, she says, to know exactly where you are.

Inside her, a child flexes, floats. It could be anywhere. It presses harder against her hand.

He is not living with Anna any more. She has his new address.

I don't know why you'd need it at the moment, he says. But I think you should have it. It's a flat. Just a rented one. It's quite nice.

I'm sorry you had to move out, she says.

He pauses and she hears the sigh come down the phone. I think it was probably for the best, he says. For us all to move on. Finally.

Maybe you're right, she says.

There is a divorce in progress. But she is careful not to ask him too much about that.

The child twists. She balances a spiral-bound pad somewhere near the baby's small, as yet unseen, knees, and apologises to her child for the indignity of using it as a writing desk. It is a small crime, considering the baby's coup of her whole body, from the mottled swell of her ankles right up to those heavy and unfamiliar breasts, but it is important for them to remain on good terms.

She knows the two of them cannot live together for much longer. She feels the first stirrings of unrest rising from within her own cells, the small, disjointed parts of her that still belong to her and her alone.

And she thinks the child feels the same. Every night, she lies awake and feels it kick against its confines. I'm sorry, she whispers. The overthrow will be painful for both of them. She hopes it will be quick.

Meanwhile, she waits. She apologises. She writes over the top of the child with soft, black words.

It is important to get it right. Of this she is certain. There is no point in setting down an account that is false from the very beginning. There will be time enough for it to become warped, passed from eye to eye, mouth to mouth. It is important to give it a chance at the truth, even if it only exists for a couple of moments before her own mind overwrites it with something more likely, more explicable, easier to tell the child swimming inside her.

She sees the black smudge on the corner of the page become the man, the man become the child inside her. She looks at the inky smear on the first finger of her left hand, and touches it gently with its right-hand twin. When she thinks of her baby, sometimes she sees the rosy white skin already marked with black fingerprints. Her pen hovers over a dark patch on the stairwell, a flicker on the wall-paper, a shadow in the folds of a dress.

Perhaps it is better to begin somewhere else. A plastic spade, a yellow bucket with ducks on the side. She puts her pen to the page to the child.

Josie drives up to see her often now. Every time she walks into the hallway, she brings something new with her, a set of miniature T-shirts, a bundle of cot sheets, a red and blue plastic rattle.

You don't have to, she says. Honestly.

But Josie is adamant. They're just little things. Little things you'll need. Trust me.

She is content to trust this mother, this new Josie who is here in her flat, who waves a bright rattle in her face, and who has slipped a blow-up mattress into the cupboard, just in case, she says, just in case.

The words she writes down are words that could have come from any of those boxes under her bed. They are words that belong in stories, not in a life she has lived. They are things that might have happened once, to a girl in a book, a girl who slipped through a book and somehow found herself inside the pages. But then the stories end, the book is closed, and the light is switched off. The girl can stay trapped inside the pages or she can fight her way free, out of the darkness and into the next morning.

She writes the words down until there are no more words to write, and then she puts the notepad away.

It'll be soon, then? he says.

Any minute now, she tells him. I'm ready to pop.

I know I've said this before, but you will call me, won't you? he says.

Of course I will, she says. As soon as there's any news, you'll be the first to know. I promise.

You sound cheerful, he says.

I am, she says. I don't know why, but I am.

I'll speak to you again soon, he says.

She hangs up and lies back on her bed, and rolls the weight of her body over into the patch of winter sunlight coming through the window. It is chilly, freshly, brightly definite.

When it finally happens, when the pain grips her, it is as if suddenly everything becomes clear. There is nothing in this world but the light and the pain and an intense hot white clarity. This is happening now, in this moment, and there is nothing that can be done to stop it. There is no escape from the pulsing and the pushing and the feel of the metal bedrail between her fingers. She sees sparks in the brightness of the ceiling.

There is no crack to slip away through here. She thinks she cries out, but she can't tell whether the sound is outside or inside the sharp, bright pain in her body.

It releases her, into an uneasy, aching pause, and she remembers her mother's hand on her back, smoothing over her spine. They have not stayed so close, like this, since she was a very small child.

Don't push until I tell you, love, a voice says – overly cheery, somewhere very far away. Don't push yet.

She can't remember what it is to push, what it is to not push. I can't, she says, I can't.

You can, another voice says, a soft, almost tender voice that mirrors the movement of the hand that is sweeping and soothing over her back. You can, says Josie. Suddenly, her mother bends forward and kisses her forearm, a brisk, unexpected kiss that makes tears start to her eyes.

Later on, there is a rush of darkness, when the pain and the pulsing become part of one, deep red-black pressure that is splitting her body apart from the inside out. She closes her eyes against the lights on the ceiling, the voices of the people around her, her mother's hand holding her own, and tries to push hard against the darkness, pressing it down and away.

At the very moment where it seems that the darkness must take her, forever, there is a sudden sting of light and heat, and then the darkness is unravelling from inside her. She gasps with the light, with the relief.

Oh bug, she hears Josie say, close to her ear. Oh bug, well done.

And then there is a first ragged squawl, a hot, heavy bundle against her chest.

A boy, says the woman placing it there. A lovely, strong, little boy. Congratulations.

She folds her arms over the weight on her breastbone and holds it close, looking down. It is a bloodied, heaving little body, with tiny features puckered up into a snarl. He is ferocious and he is bright and he is alive, so alive.

She looks at him, lying there, and cannot quite believe he exists. He scrunches up his mouth into another yowl, and she presses her lips to his forehead, and tastes her blood, their blood. It is a new, fierce magic she has not expected.

*

He stands in the doorway. I hope you don't mind, but when I got the call I had to come, he says. I couldn't not.

She makes some attempt to smooth down her hair, adjust the neck of her gown, push herself up straighter against the crinkling sheet and pillows. I don't mind, she says, and it is the truth. I don't mind at all.

Josie tells me all went well, he says. With everything. And – the boy.

Did you see her outside?

Just now, he says. In the hall. She said to come straight in.

He stays still, and does not step on to the space of white tiles between them, where the light hits the floor and catches her eye in a cluster of sparks. He is cradling a bundle of tulips, blazing red and yellow in his arm. She rests her hand on the side of the plastic box beside her.

Well, come in, then, she says.

He hesitates, and then it is the sparks that finally seem to propel the long, grey narrowness of him forward, past the point where the light dances on the floor and on into the space behind it. He comes closer, and the lights flicker above them and then it is just the two of them, in front of the neat white plastic box, a sleeping pink creature inside.

Look, she says, look. He puts the tulips down on the bed beside her.

The child is in her arms, the child is in his arms, it opens its marble eyes. She sits up on the bed and watches the two faces come closer together, each marked by their own peculiar wrinkles.

Like seaglass, he says. The tiny eyes balance in their sockets so perfectly. He turns his son towards him in the crook of his elbow, and touches one small, flexing finger. His own hand, unbidden, mirrors the curl and lift.

In the Shadows

And there is one more thing, which seems as good a place to end as any.

It is a girl, sitting alone, in one room stacked among many others in a big, brick block of clustered lives. She has come home from the island early, for reasons that she will not want to talk to her friends about when school starts again next week. When her mother makes phone calls, she has taken to closing the door to the kitchen, and when she is not on the phone, she hovers over the girl in an awkward way that makes them both feel fretful and sad.

It is only when her mother has gone to sleep, or at least to her bedroom to pace up and down on the creak of the floorboards, that the girl can be entirely on her own. She gets out of bed, kneels and reaches into the corner, hoping the dark will gather around her.

It does not happen every time now, not like it did before. Yes, some nights the darkness still agrees to take her hand with a tentative, electric shake, but some nights it merely quivers over the tip of her finger, and on others still it stays flat and hard and resolutely wooden. She has stopped keeping her notebooks there for fear that one day she might never be able to retrieve them.

Tonight, the corner seems to be set in an unusually deep, black cloud, which sends the thrill chasing through her body and catching at her chest. She stretches out her fingers, and they tingle as they disappear. Daring, she thrusts her whole hand in and turns her wrist, first one way, then the other. Her knuckles graze against the fizzing dark.

There is a sudden, unseen flurry and something feathery brushes against her palm, skating over it like a spider. Before she has a chance to think about it, she has snatched her hand back into the real, comforting gloom of the room, and the corner becomes straight and solid again.

That might have been all, of course. Except that when she wakes up the next morning, she looks again at the walls in daylight. The corner itself is just as it has ever been, two crudely joined strips of white-painted skirting, one with a knothole stain seeping through into a pale brown ring under the varnish. But lying on the carpet beside it is something bright and unexpected – a smoothly frosted green circle, the size of a coin. She picks it up to examine it.

No doubt about it, it is a perfect piece of glass, a real treasure stone.

Acknowledgements

Thank you to all at Arcadia, especially my editor Helen Francis, Joe Harper, and Angeline Rothermundt. Thank you to Lucy Dundas and Cassie Lawrence at Flint. Thank you to Michael Arditti and Dan Mogford.

Thank you to my agent, Karolina Sutton at Curtis Brown, for all her support and championship.

I owe a debt of thanks dating back many years to the works of C.S. Lewis, Susan Cooper and Diana Wynne Jones, without which this book would never have come about.

There are so many people who have helped me during the writing and publication process, with wise advice, early reading, cheerleading, patience and, when necessary, gin. I am terrified I have left one of you out. Thank you so much Kat Brown, Rachael Beale, Nina Douglas, Jessica Leigh, Harriet Mann, Layla Rodham, Nathalie Tamam, Elizabeth Corbishley, Barbara Cooke, Helen Hildebrand, Thomas Truong, Laura Coffey, Lucy Pearson, James Kay, Amanda Emslie, Ciara Daly, Nicola Gover and the Pocket Friends. Thank you, Benjamin Johncock.

Finally, thank you always to my family, in particular my father Edward, my mother Katherine and my brother Matt, both for love and unfailing support throughout, and also for island summers and seaglass.